MIDLIFE DO OVER
A LATER IN LIFE HIGH SCHOOL SWEETHEART ROMANCE

PIPER SULLIVAN

Copyright © 2022 by Piper Sullivan

All rights reserved.

No part of this book may be reproduced in any form or by any electronic or mechanical means, including information storage and retrieval systems, without written permission from the author, except for the use of brief quotations in a book review.

Sign up to my Exclusive Romance Connoisseurs' Club to receive my Free Romance, Her Fake Fiancé Billionaire Boss.

PROLOGUE

Pippa ~ 2 Months Ago

"Thank you for visiting Graze today. I hope you had a wonderful meal." I flashed my most dazzling smile at the clearly less than impressed couple, waiting patiently for them to speak.

The couple stared at each other with a worried expression before the woman turned to me. "The asparagus was delicious, buttery and perfectly firm. The mashed potatoes were a little bland, and the steak was just okay. But we didn't want to complain."

That would be a first for the crowd Graze drew on a daily basis. "Feedback is always welcome," I assured them with a friendly grin.

"That's not a goddamn julienne! Open your eyes or get the hell out of my kitchen."

I kept my smile tight while the couple listened in

clear horror as Chef Rodrick unleashed yet another tirade on a kitchen employee. "He has high standards." It was the best I could do to attempt a defense of the chef's unacceptable behavior, but the couple's eyes went wide, and they hurried out of the restaurant. Probably never to return.

Oh well.

Chef Rodrick had been on a tirade all shift, verbally abusing the kitchen staff, barking angrily at the waitstaff as if they were the reason his food was coming out of the kitchen in substandard quality. He had the temperamental and egotistical parts of being a professional chef down to a science. It was just too bad that his food fell flat if everything didn't go perfectly, which it never ever did in a professional kitchen. He'd been hired at Graze almost a year ago, and frankly, I didn't know how he still had a job except for he could be charming when reporters were around and he was easy on the eyes.

Too bad he's not easy on the ears.

I was the front of house manager for Graze, had been for the past three years, but it was only the past twelve months that had been a hellish nightmare. But Rodrick was a star, allegedly anyway, which meant the rest of us had to grin and pretend as if the kitchen wasn't run by a complete psychopath.

"Excuse me, miss?"

I let out a sigh at the one title no woman over the age

of forty wanted to hear. Miss. It just felt like a commentary on my sadly single-in-the-city status. Chicago was a city of almost nine million people, and I couldn't find one solid, single man to date. But that wasn't the customer's fault, so I turned with a mostly professional grin and headed to table three, located near the front windows with a view of Michigan Avenue. "What can I do for you folks today?" I glanced around the table and did a double take at the man with the silver goatee who I was pretty sure was the famed restaurant critic Paul Renault. He could make or break a restaurant with a few taps of his keyboard.

"How was the leg of lamb?"

The woman with a short black bob and a pinched expression answered for the table. "Not good, sweetie."

I gave my obligatory frown and nodded. "I'm so sorry to hear that, what can I do to make your dining experience better?"

"We'd like a new lamb, cooked properly this time. Please."

"Absolutely, I'll let the chef know. Would you like a complimentary glass of champagne while you wait?"

"Absolutely," the man I was pretty sure was Paul Renault replied with a relieved groan.

With a polite nod, I turned away from the table and headed towards the kitchen. Before I pushed through the swinging doors, I sucked in a deep breath and let it out slowly, reaching for a calm I didn't feel knowing that an interaction with Rodrick was imminent.

You got this. Even if you don't, it's your job.

My little pep talk did nothing to stop my racing heart, so I did what I always did when times got tough, I stood a little taller, pushed my shoulders back before I balanced the platter of lamb in my hands, and forged ahead. The kitchen was a beautiful sort of chaos, the way all pro kitchens were. It was that song and dance that had drew me to the world of fine dining, this craziness that produced the most delicious, beautiful, artistic edible creations known to man. I loved it.

Usually.

"Get the hell out of my kitchen! Now!" Chef Rodrick's roared words didn't intimidate me in the least, but the rest of the kitchen fell mute.

This will be a lot easier since he shouted at me first, I told myself as I fixed a bland expression on my face, the platter resting on my palms. Being nice to Rodrick never paid off anyway.

"Gladly. As soon as I let you know that this leg of lamb is dry."

If possible, the kitchen fell even quieter as the chef whirled around, his whites still pristine after hours of working, and sucked in a breath.

"Excuse me?" The disbelief that he could have possibly cooked a dish imperfectly was laughable given the complaints I fielded this shift.

Instead of using the diplomacy I always tried for when dealing with sensitive and temperamental chefs, I smiled. "As dry as the Sahara."

Rodrick laughed. "I don't have time for your silly games, Pippa. Go back to the front of the house and worry about doing *your* job."

Dear Lord help me find my calm. I let out an exhausted sigh and stared at him in those deep green eyes. "Table three wants another lamb because this one is dry. So *dry* they couldn't eat but a few bites each." I put extra emphasis on the word dry because that vein in the middle of his forehead was already pulsing and that amused me. "Just fix it because-,"

He cut me off before I could tell him who the lamb was meant for. "My lamb is not fucking dry. I don't cook anything dry, so go back out there and tell your precious customers that's how the lamb is cooked." Rodrick shook his head and swiped a dismissive hand in my direction. "Just stay in your own damn lane, Pippa."

I nodded, not at all unaccustomed to chef's belittling my work, as if dealing with the customers wasn't as important as the food they ate. "Whatever. You do what you want Rodrick, but the customers who paid for this leg of lamb says it's too dry to eat." I held up the platter and the sous chef moved to relieve me of the heavy piece of meat, until Rodrick held up a hand to stop him.

"Tell them to try it again."

I shook my head. "Maybe you should try it, because they did, and it was, quote, *not good*."

"That's not possible."

"That's funny, because to those three customers it's more than possible, it's reality." Reality that they overpaid for what amounted to lamb jerky, from their perspective.

Another bark of laughter sounded, this time derisive, and I knew another tirade was coming. "This coming from some backwoods hillbilly who's spent a little time in fine dining establishments? Excuse me if I don't bow down to your culinary expertise."

"No, excuse me for thinking a chef might pull out a meat thermometer when all the customers say their steaks are too dry, or too rare. It's not my culinary expertise they come for, it's yours, and lately that is in serious question." I was done arguing with this idiot who clearly didn't have the sense the good lord gave him.

"Yeah?" Rodrick stood at six-foot-four and decided to use his considerable height advantage against me, looming above me as if I was supposed to be scared.

My heart raced, but I ignored it, too fired up to worry that today might be the day he lost it completely. "Yeah. Everything tonight has been overcooked as hell, but you're incapable of taking any kind of criticism, so no one tells you, and the waitstaff gets stiffed on good tips. Because of you. Not some backwoods hillbilly, but the allegedly classically trained man-child dressed in his chef's costume."

"Take it back," he growled.

"Get out of my face, Rodrick."

He smiled because he knew he had me at a disadvantage with the cumbersome platter of meat in my hands. "If I don't?"

I set the platter down on the expediting strip and turned to face him. "I'm not one of your kitchen slaves, I bite back." I shook my head and took a step away, not in defeat, but retreat.

Rodrick's hand reached out and grabbed my arm, causing a collective gasp among the kitchen staff. "Get your hands off me, Rodrick." My heart thudded against my chest as my flight or fight instinct kicked in. "Let. Me. Go."

"Don't walk away from me."

"Get your damn hands off me. I won't tell you again." He laughed and gave my arm a tight squeeze, a look of utter glee in his green eyes. He was getting off on hurting me and the yelp I let out when he squeezed even tighter, pushed me into action. "Ow!"

"Right," he snorted. "Or what?"

What happened next, in hindsight, was ill-advised at best, but I was a southern girl at heart, and no one got to lay hands on me without paying the consequences. I grabbed the leg of lamb and swung it at Rodrick, hitting him right in his stupid, smug face. He hit the ground with a grunt. "Or you'll regret it."

He smiled up at me. "I regret nothing. You're done here. Pack up your shit and get out."

I smiled down at him and shook my head. "Maybe so, but that lamb you refused to make again? Was ordered by Paul Renault. Good luck getting your next job." Without another word, I turned on my bright red heels and returned to the dining room.

At the end of my shift, I finished up my responsibilities and called my best friend, Valona, who still lived in our hometown of Carson Creek, Tennessee. "Hey Val, it's me.

There was a moment of silence before she spoke. "Pippa. What's wrong?"

"Other than the fact that my chef is the world's biggest jackass? Not much." I gave her an abbreviated version of the shift from hell and sighed with exhaustion. "He actually said, *you're done here.*"

"Pippa, what if he's serious?" Valona was a natural worrier, about anything and everyone in her orbit. As a single mother to my adorable goddaughters, she didn't stop worrying even when she was asleep.

"Oh he was, but Rodrick doesn't have the power to fire me. That doesn't mean I won't get fired, just that I'm not yet."

"What are you going to do if you get fired?"

I let out a frustrated sigh. "What do you want me to

do, Val? He grabbed my arm and squeezed it. Hard. Twice."

"You did the right thing, but what will you do if you lose this job?"

"I'll figure it out." The same way I figured out my life when I was eighteen and the future I thought I would have, vanished right before my eyes. "Hang on, another call's coming in. Wish me luck."

"Good luck, honey. Love you."

"Thanks." A deep breath and I switched to what I was sure was The Call. "Hello?"

"Pippa." I recognized Josh Wiseman's nasally voice immediately. "You hit Rodrick with a leg of lamb."

"He grabbed my arm and hurt me, Josh. He had no right to put his hands on me."

"I agree, Pippa, but I can't keep you on. You understand?"

I nodded, nostrils flaring as my anger built. "Yeah, you think he's the next big celebrity chef. But let me tell you, Paul Renault might disagree with you."

"What does that mean?"

"You'll find out when the rest of Chicago does."

Josh sighed. "Let's not make this ugly."

"Oh, I won't make it ugly, honey. Trust me." I let out a sigh and flashed a smile at myself in the rearview mirror. "But my lawyer might."

"I wouldn't do that if I were you."

"Yeah? Well I wouldn't keep an abusive prick on staff who is a lawsuit waiting to happen. Talk soon, Josh."

"Valona, you there?"

"I'm here. Are you fired?"

"Yep. And I'm suing. Wish me luck." Lord knows I'm gonna need it.

CHAPTER 1
RYAN

One Month Ago

I looked around my hometown after being away on tour for the past ten months, and smiled. Carson Creek was as small town as small towns came, complete with a Main Street lined with big red oaks, wooden sidewalks and American flags flowing in the wind on every business. Colorful awnings, sale signs, and people actually chatting with their neighbors.

Carson Creek was home. Had been since the day I was born and no matter how far I traveled, what I had experienced on the road, it would always be home. Home. The word took on new meaning when you spent most of the year touring the country, and the world. Things that used to bother me, the gossip, the way everyone was all up in everyone else's business, the lack of secrets and late night delivery, suddenly seemed charming. Even endearing.

That's why I did what I did. I had taken a step to ensure that my stay in Carson Creek would be permanent. I bought a restaurant. What in the hell did I know about restaurants? Nothing at all. I was a simple man who preferred burgers and fries, steak and potatoes to things like sushi and fine wine. But I was a quick study, had learned to play the guitar on my own as well as the piano, and became a pretty good songwriter without any professional training.

Most of all, I had time. The tour would be over soon, which meant I could focus on writing the next album and learning the ins and outs of running a successful restaurant.

I maneuvered the car to the dead end street that led to the Old Country House property where my restaurant was located. The long driveway was reminiscent of those big old properties where generations of families lived at the same time, except this was an oversized events' venue, which provided the restaurant with guaranteed business. From a business perspective it was a smart move to make, and my name recognition would—hopefully—help increase bookings.

It was just how Carson Creek worked, everyone chipped in to help out everyone else.

Damn, it's good to be home.

The long entrance split into three roads, the one on

the left led to Dark Horse, the restaurant was named after the first song I wrote that went double platinum. It was my biggest achievement at the time, considering Derek was the lead singer and Roman was the showman. It was still my pride and joy, played at bars all over the world, drunk patrons singing along with my lyrics about being underestimated by a love interest.

And now it was a living breathing thing. A place that was just mine, not The Gregory Brothers.

I stepped from my Jeep that was older than dirt, and smiled at the sight of Mayor Carson, arms folded but smiling broadly. "Ryan Gregory. Good to see you." He extended a hand to me and I accepted it with a grin of my own.

"Still weird that you're the mayor, but it's good to see you too, Chase." I still remembered him as my girlfriend's pipsqueak little brother with his nose stuck in a book.

"It's my third term, Ryan, about time you got used to it. Especially now that you're a business owner." He nodded over his shoulder to the brick building with Dark Horse scrawled across the front, complete with a Stetson wearing stallion as the logo, even though I was no damn cowboy.

"Third term, huh? Good for you."

Chase rolled his eyes. "You donated to my campaign, Ryan."

"Me? Can't be true." I shrugged it off because the kid

was good at his job. I didn't spend much time in Carson Creek these days, but the gossip still managed to reach me.

"How's it feel to be back in town? You've been gone a while this time."

I nodded, acknowledging the truth of his words. "Been too long if you ask me, but this tour is major for us." After so long in the game, it was a gift to be so popular, to adjust to the digital age of music and streaming, after two decades in the business. "Feels strange, but good to be back, which pretty much sums up life in Carson Creek." It was always an odd mix of relief to be someplace familiar, and anxiety about being around people who knew everything about you.

Chase laughed and shook his head. "A sentiment I understand completely." He clapped me on the back and there it was, that sense of relief that came whenever Chase was kind to me. Civil. His sister hadn't forgiven me for leaving to pursue my dreams. Still.

"I'm excited to come back for an extended stay once the tour is over, though."

The sound of heels clacking behind me drew my attention to Margo Blanchard-Devereaux, the owner of The Old Country House, the business and the actual house. She wore a pale pink suit with matching heels, walking at a fast clip as if she was always in a hurry.

"Ryan. Mayor. Sorry I'm late, I had a panicking bride to deal with." Type A to the core, Margot smoothed over her pristine clothes and hair with a sigh. "Good to have you back, Ryan."

"Temporarily," I added with a smile for an old friend.

She flashed a proud smile, the one I'd gotten used to over the years as the whole town took pride in the success of the wild Gregory brothers. "How's the tour going? I read somewhere that the last two weeks sold out in just minutes."

"Yeah, the crowds have been amazing." It's not that I was uncomfortable talking about my work, my songs and music, but touring was part of the job. Enjoyable for the fans who came to hear the live version, to sing along and have a good time. Ticket sales was for the studio to worry about.

The conversation fell flat, and Margot, never one to endure awkward silences, clapped her hands briskly. "I'm excited to see the inside of this place. Your assistant has been very tight-lipped," she added with a frown. "Very."

I laughed. "Devon is efficient and loyal." My assistant didn't do anything he didn't want to unless it was about protecting my image and privacy, and I'd given explicit instructions that I wanted to see the finished product first.

"Yes, well, he is that," she added haughtily and looked up at the restaurant sign with a frown. "I still wish you would have chosen a different name. One that's more customer friendly."

I sighed, wondering if the built-in business would be worth the hassle of Margot's constant needling. The woman had to have everything her way or she fell apart, but this was my baby. My business. "I can always find another location so you won't have to see such an eyesore, Margot."

She blinked in shock, eyes growing round at my harsh words because everyone in town went out of their way to be polite, even when it wasn't warranted. Recovering quickly, Margot brushed off my words with a smile. "Just some friendly advice."

"From your long tenure in the restaurant business?"

Margot was saved from scrambling for an explanation when the doors of Dark Horse opened and Devon appeared, with a welcoming smile for everyone except Margot. "Looks like we have a crowd." His questioning gaze slid to mine, and I knew he was wondering if this group counted as me laying eyes on the restaurant first.

"It's fine," I assured him with a sigh. I wanted time to look at the place on my own, to give it a thorough examination so I could sit with it, figure out if it was what I wanted for my first foray into real world investments. "Input is always welcome. So is word of mouth promotions," I added with a grin.

Satisfied, Devon nodded and took a step back to wave us all inside. He hung back and fell into step beside me. "I've hired an amazing chef who is the perfect blend of modern fine dining and southern home cooking. She's from Knoxville, but trained in New York and Italy. She's also provided me with a mile-long list of kitchen staff." Devon nodded to the stack of papers on the bar. "I've got more applications than I can handle, which brings me to the most important hiring decision. Front of House manager."

I paused and quirked a smile at him. "More important than the chef?"

Devon shrugged. "Good food doesn't matter if the service is crappy or there aren't enough waitresses to meet demand."

"Good point." One I hadn't thought about. "What do you need from me?"

Devon froze and stared at me like I'd grown a third eye. "This person will have to be someone you trust, someone you can get along with, especially if you plan to stick around for the foreseeable future."

Oh. Right. "Make sure it's a local who knows how things work around here. Someone with restaurant experience and someone who won't just say yes to me even when I don't know what the hell I'm talking about."

"Seriously? You want me to hire the person for this position?"

"Why not? You hired the chef."

"That's because you wouldn't know good food if it jumped off the plate and bit you." His smile softened his harsh, but true, words. "You can sample her cooking if you're curious."

"I will, but later though. I trust you."

"This place is stunning," Margot practically shouted across the empty dining room.

At her words, I was finally able to give the place my full attention. Devon had done his damnedest to bring my vision to life, and he'd succeeded beyond my wildest dreams. The Dark Horse dining room was a strange mix of old school saloon and modern fine dining with dark wood tables and matching floors, the long bar was a shade darker than the other wood finishes, drawing the eye first. The chairs were heavy with burgundy leather upholstery and decorative wooden studs instead of metal or brass. Dim lighting gave the place a cool, exclusive feel and the fancy wiry chandeliers that hung above each table let you know this was a place where you could expect great food for your money.

"Well? Don't leave me hanging, boss."

I smiled at Devon. "I love it."

"You do?" He looked around and pointed at the mirrored bar stacked six shelves high, the leather stools bolted to the floor in front of the bar. The wildflowers inside small wooden vases in the center of each table. "You love it?"

"Yeah," I sighed. "I wouldn't have picked this stuff myself. Hell, I wouldn't have known to pick it, but it all works. You did a good job, Devon. A really good job."

His shoulders sank in relief. "I'm glad to hear that."

"I'm happier to be able to say it." There was so much that went into opening a restaurant and I didn't know half of what I needed to, not yet, but I would. As soon as the tour was over and I came home for good. "What are we looking at for opening day?"

"A month or two? First I have to hire a manager and together we'll have to hire front of house staff, settle the menu and specials. Shouldn't be too long after you get back."

I did a double take at his words. "Me? Why do I have to be around for that?"

"Because, Dark Horse, you are the main attraction. People will show up just for a chance to lay eyes on the quietest Gregory brother, and hopefully they'll stay for a steak, a bottle of whiskey or a three course meal."

Ah, dammit. "Right." It was high time I got used to being part of the sideshow. I'd spent my entire career doing it in the background, happy to let Derek and Roman soak up the spotlight. But this business was mine, which meant the song and dance for customers was mine to perform.

It was a small price to pay for a much-needed distraction from the fact that I was getting too old to be on tour nonstop.

CHAPTER 2
PIPPA

Today

"It shouldn't have come down to this, Pippa." Josh sat across a small table and looked at me with disappointed eyes, a look that had, for years, compelled me to work harder and longer hours, to do my absolute best to impress him. Today that look only fired up the anger that had mostly subsided over the past two months. "If you had just let me fire you and left quietly, you'd still be able to work in this town."

I laughed. "Oh please, Josh. Don't act like I'm the only one that took a big hit with your attempts to blackball me. Sure some of the chefs who prefer to run their kitchens with a heavy dose of abuse don't want to deal with me, but how many restaurants want to hire your former golden boy?" I looked at my lawyer who sat beside me with a stoic expression and shook my head. "I mean, it's lunchtime in downtown, and there are what, maybe five tables occupied today? Seems to me you fired the wrong person."

"Graze will be just fine."

"Eventually. This town has a long memory, especially when powerful men gang up on a woman just protecting herself from physical abuse." This town, I learned the hard way, also had a low tolerance for tattletales, which apparently I was. Twelve interviews in two months had resulted in nine different versions of, "don't call us, we'll call you." Three at least had the guts to tell me they didn't want the publicity of hiring the infamous Leg of Lamb Lady.

It was all vague promises that meant nothing, which meant I was done in Chicago.

Josh smiled smugly. "I've had a few calls for references."

"Yeah and you told them nothing but lies. Thanks for that." I held my hand out in a *gimme* motion. "I'll have my checks now, though."

That wiped the stupid smug smile on his face. "Hope this money is worth the damage you caused."

"You made your choice first, Josh. Remember that. When this place starts to circle the drain, think about the fact that you were happy to keep a man with a history of physically abusing his employees, his coworkers and his girlfriends, over a loyal employee. I hope that thought keeps you warm at night."

Josh let out a long, exhausted sigh that told me I'd hit the mark. "Severance," he said and pushed the check across the table. "And settlement check."

"Thanks. And I won't hold it against you that you tried to make me homeless by withholding my severance pay for two months. But I will wish upon the first shootin' star I see that you get exactly what you have coming to ya. Later." I pushed away from the table and turned on my heels, stoic attorney at my side, and walked away with my head held high.

"You did great."

The attorney speaks! I looked up at him with a wide grin and held out my hand. "Thank you, Mr. Griffith. You made this entire process less scary than I imagined."

There was a flash of a smile on his lips before it disappeared. "You didn't need my help, but this case put me on the radar of the partners, so thank you."

"Good luck."

"Same to you." Inside the parking garage, we went our separate ways and I ignored the shakiness of my legs and let out a long sigh as I looked over the railing and out to the city, gray and drizzling. Even horrible weather couldn't stop Chicago from moving forward. It was one of the things I loved about this place. It's why I'd made it my second home. Fifteen years, three fine dining establishments and one chain restaurant job under my belt, but now I was leaving this place behind.

It didn't feel right to leave under these conditions,

but thanks to Paul Renault, the whole city knew the truth, that I wasn't some emotionally abusive basket case. A hot head, he'd called me, which was just as bad for a front of house manager, so it was still the kiss of death. Temporarily, anyway. So, instead of working my way back up in this city, I decided to leave. To pack up my bags, my apartment, my whole life and head back home, to Carson Creek.

Tennessee here I come!

I hadn't been home in more than five years. It was too risky. My heart still too fragile. More than twenty years had passed since the love of my life had told me he was leaving town, without me, and still it was too raw. It didn't help that memories of him were all over the town. Wild child made good was a great redemption story in a town that craved a happy ending.

Now, avoidance was, well unavoidable. I could only hope that luck was on my side and he was on some stage on the other side of the world. Of course, he would be back—eventually—and I would deal with that, with him when the time came.

But on top of my priority list was finding a job. A place to live and a paycheck. At forty, I was right back where I started. No, I was worse off than when I was a brokenhearted eighteen year old, because at least then I was running towards a new future, a new life. A new, unknown adventure.

Now I just felt as if I was moving in reverse. Going

back home with no job, no prospects for a job, divorced after a short-lived marriage, and my tail between my legs. It felt like failure.

A big fat freakin' failure.

Ten hours and only two bathroom breaks later, I rolled past the Welcome to Carson Creek sign and felt the knot in my belly grow tighter with each passing block. Each southern red oak tugged my smile a little brighter, and my belly a bit more anxiety-filled. This was my home and I missed it terribly.

So much, that every sign of familiarity made my heart ache, clench with regret that I let one little heartache keep me away for so long. I missed years with my best friend because phone calls, emails and video calls just weren't enough. Not when my goddaughters were growing like weeds and growing into their personalities.

As I pulled up to Valona's three story Victorian, I smiled, suddenly very happy to be back home. To be with the people who knew me best in the world, my best friend and my brother, once again. They knew me, knew my heart, and had been with me during the best and worst moments of my life. Despite my absences, they didn't hold it against me, and most of all, both had welcomed me back with open arms.

And I would reward them by not being a burden or a distraction from their busy lives. I would spend a night or two with Valona and the girls, catching up and loving on my bestie and her sweet girls, and when I woke up tomorrow I would get started on the rest of my life. Starting with a home of my own and a job.

Not necessarily in that order, but a big fat failure couldn't be too picky.

CHAPTER 3
RYAN

"Holy shit man, that was the greatest show on Earth!" My youngest brother, Roman, clapped me on the back as we rushed off stage after a third encore, and made our way down the well-lit tunnel until we reached the main door of the backstage area. "That was the shit, and you know it! Don't even bother denying it." Roman entered the room, not at all nonplussed by all the women, the strangers lounging among our stuff as if they belonged.

It was still unnerving to me, but I was a little older than Roman's thirty-three years. He still found joy and escape in slipping it inside of a random chick anywhere there was a modicum of privacy. I didn't judge him for how he chose to unwind, it just didn't do it for me anymore.

Unfortunately.

While Roman got sucked into the clutches of two wannabe groupies, I sat back, feeling good as I watched the partiers wearing wide smiles as if they had any claim on the kickass performance we put on tonight. For my part, I felt bittersweet, the same way I felt when we finished recording an album, performed the last day of a tour, ended a relationship. It was all just another ending to me, good while it lasted, but there was no desire to go back once it was over.

Except that once.

Derek and Roman soaked up the attention, as they always did. Whether it was women or genuine fans, they ate up every moment of it. Not as if it were their due, but as if it could all go away at any minute. Derek had a rapt audience as he recounted the way he felt when all fifty thousand concert goers sang along with him to *Always In My Heart,* while Roman whispered sweet nothings to a redhead and accepted small promising kisses from a blond.

I sat back the way I always did, and observed every little detail. Not in a creepy way, at least not to me, but I was a people watcher. It helped me write songs and stay grounded.

And now, I was ready to get the hell off the road. To sleep in my own bed with the brand new memory foam mattress, every night. It was a luxury I'd learned years ago to never take for granted, the pleasure of lying down on the same pillow in the same bed night after night.

There was a certain sense of comfort in that kind of sameness, and no place offered that level of comfort, of sameness, as Carson Creek. It was home, it was where I could unwind, enjoy and just soak up the beauty of the place, let it soothe my restless heart. Let it inspire me.

That was my goal for my stay at home, to write songs for the new album, to relax, and learn all that I could about the ins and outs of running a restaurant. It wasn't exactly the rock star behavior people expected, but thankfully I was the boring brother. The quiet one. The old one. *Old, my ass. Forty wasn't old, not for me. I felt better today than when I was thirty, damn those bloggers.*

"Hey man, watching everyone like a creeper instead of enjoying the last night of the tour?" Roman's deep voice, filled with amusement, slowly pulled me from my thoughts, my plans for the future.

I shrugged off his gentle ribbing. "It's what I do."

"Luckily, you're almost as hot as me, or else it would be damn creepy." Roman laughed again and pulled a cold beer from a nearby cooler and shook his head as he twisted the top and took a long sip.

I let out a sharp bark of laughter at our familiar banter. "You wish you were as hot as me. Maybe after your balls drop, you'll come close." Roman flipped me off, as he always did, and then handed me a beer.

"What are your plans now that the tour is over?"

Good question. I hadn't told either of my brothers about my new investment. "Carson Creek. Maybe a few changes to my house, writing for the next album, and keeping a close eye on my new investment."

Roman's blue eyes widened. "A new investment and you didn't consult me? Or Derek?" He let out a low whistle. "I think I'm offended."

"Don't be. It's a restaurant, not your thing."

"Not *my* thing? This coming from the guy who lives on peanut butter and jelly rather than trying carpaccio or kale." He shook his head, slapping his knee as he was overcome with laughter. "Not my jam, but if any one of us could make it work, it's you." I gave him a *don't bullshit a bullshitter* look and Roman chuckled. "I mean it. You're so serious and those lyrics that have sustained us all these years, they come from a deep thinker. Not shallow pricks like me and Derek."

He wasn't wrong, but I knew my baby brother better than I knew anyone else in the world. I'd taken care of him when our Mama died weeks after giving birth to him. Changed his dirty diapers, taught him how to walk and how to charm a woman. And yeah, he was definitely up to something.

"All right, drop the shit, Ro and tell me what you want."

A loud guffaw of a laugh erupted from his rangy frame, tugging a reluctant smile across my own face. "Me? Your baby brother, and I can't even compliment you at the end of the longest tour known to mankind without suspicion? Now I *know* I'm offended."

I rolled my eyes because Roman wasn't a cruel man, but he wasn't a serious man either. "What do you want, Ro?"

He sighed and stared at the packed backstage area, his eyes landing on everyone but not really seeing anyone in particular. "I want to do a solo album." He let the words hang in the air for a long time, like he was waiting for me to explode or talk him out of it. I kept silent. "I don't want to leave the band, but I want to do more. Our next album isn't due for a year, what the hell am I supposed to do with all that free time aside from get myself into trouble?" He laughed. "You think I'm an asshole?"

"Nah." I shook my head and turned to look at my brother, really look at him. "I think you know that you don't do well with a lot of downtime and if you want a career away from us, you should go for it."

"Seriously?"

"Yeah, seriously. As you love to remind me, you're young with a lot of life ahead of you. You tell Derek your plans yet?"

His blue eyes, identical to mine and Derek's, and our older sister Lacey, widened almost comically. "You kidding? I want to enjoy this last night of the tour, possibly my life. I'm telling you because," he sighed again and turned to me.

"Don't keep me in suspense, Roman."

"It would mean a lot to me if you wrote some songs

for me. For my voice." He flashed a smug smile at my surprised expression. "See? I was being totally genuine with my compliments."

I couldn't deny that Roman's words floored me. Not that I lacked confidence in my ability as a songwriter, just that, I guess I never let myself think too hard about what my brothers thought of my skills. "Me?"

"Hell yeah," he nodded and took another swig from his beer. "Who else?"

"Literally anyone else. Nashville is filled with songwriters looking for their big break."

"Yeah, but they don't have the depth that you do, and they don't know my voice better than the man who taught me to sing and play the drums." He looked at me, hope and expectation darkening his blue eyes. "What do you think?"

I didn't know what to think, but the truth was I could use all the distractions I could get over the next few months, and Roman was my baby brother, practically a son to me. "Ask me again in a week after I've had time to relax and unwind, you know, after the longest tour known to mankind."

His face pulled into a wide, satisfied grin. "Thanks, Ry."

"I didn't say yes."

"No, but you didn't say no, and we both know that means you're halfway to yes."

"We'll see." He was right, but he was too smug for

his own good, and it was good for him to wait, to sweat it out before getting the answer he wanted to hear.

"All right, fine," he conceded. "I'll be knocking on your door in a week. One week, Ry."

"Not a moment sooner," I told him as he pushed off the seat beside me and sauntered back over the stacked redhead with the hungry green eyes and blonde with the pouty lips and barely there dress.

I stood soon after, grabbed a bottle whiskey from the table and left the backstage area and the concert venue, sparing one final, wistful glance at the perfect send-off. Without a word to my brothers, I made my way back to the hotel and slept peacefully, knowing it would be the last hotel bed I slept in for months.

CHAPTER 4
PIPPA

"The first thing on my list is to find a job." It felt ridiculous, no, it felt pathetic to be starting over at forty years old, but this was my reality and I was determined to make the best of it. "A restaurant job would be ideal, but at this point I need to start earning some money."

Valona's big sage green eyes narrowed in confusion. "I thought you just got your severance pay and a big fat settlement."

"I have it and it's going in the bank today, well as soon as I have an actual address. But I can't live off that money forever, Val." As far as I could tell, there still weren't many restaurants in Carson Creek. It had given us the perfect excuse to make the hour long drive into Nashville every weekend as teens. "I was hoping to stay here, but if that's not possible, there's no point searching for a house."

"There is an option, but I'm not sure if you're gonna like it." Valona's face was etched with worry.

"I'm listening. Tell me everything."

Valona nodded and got up from the kitchen table, her long legs taking a direct path to the coffee pot which she brought back to the table. "There's a property on Mulligrew Drive called The Old Country House."

"That overgrown eyesore on the dead end street?" That place had served as fodder for our childhood imaginations, and then a semi-secret place where we could drink and kiss boys when we shouldn't have been.

"That's the one. It's no longer overgrown or an eyesore. Margot bought it and turned it into a whole events complex."

"Like a wedding venue?" I shook my head. "I don't want to oversee caterers, Val. Is that even a job?"

She smiled and shook her head. "This is much bigger than that. Margot owns the land and the gorgeous plantation house the property is named for, so she gets a cut of everything. Carlotta Montgomery is the event planner. She specializes in weddings, but she does it all from debutante balls to bar mitzvah parties, bachelor parties and even divorce parties. I take photos for the events, usually on the property, but sometimes the couples want engagement photos and when I find studio space, I'll do them there when the situation calls for it." She smiled proudly, and it was downright contagious.

"That's great, Val! It's like guaranteed business for your new business."

"Thanks," she answered shyly, a small blush staining her cheeks. "Anyway, there's a restaurant on the property that's open to the public, but will also be used for events. The place is new and in search of a manager."

That was music to my ears and I felt excitement pulse through my veins. "Seriously?"

Valona nodded.

"Way to bury the lead, woman!" I reached for my phone at the end of the table. "What's the name of this place." Valona was silent and I looked up with a question in my eyes. "Well?"

She nibbled her bottom lip before pushing the words from her mouth. "It's called Dark Horse."

"Cool name. Is it some type of saloon? Never mind, found it." The photos of the place were spectacular, decorated in dark wood and burgundy leather. "It's fine dining?"

"It is, with a bit of a rustic flair."

My leg started to bounce excitedly. "Val, if I get this job then I can stay here in town, spend more time with you and the girls." What are the odds that a fine dining restaurant would open up in small town Tennessee just as I was looking for a job in fine dining? "It's kismet," I declared and stood up. "I have to go there. Right now. Is this a situation where you have to know the right people?"

"As far as I know you can show up with your resume. But Pippa, there's something you should know."

"I have to find something to wear. Something that looks like I'm a pro, but that I can fit in with the people of Carson Creek."

Valona laughed. "You *are* the people of Carson Creek, Pippa Carson."

"You know what I mean. I haven't lived here in a long time and some might consider me too citified." I stopped in the doorway and waved Valona along. "Come help me pick out something to wear. Please?"

"Fine, but there's something you should know about Dark Horse."

I waved off her concern with a literal swipe of my hand. "Nothing can be as bad as dealing with Rodrick."

"I wouldn't be so sure about that," she mumbled, but I was already heading down the first floor hall to the guest room.

Inside my room, I pulled open the first suitcase I found, relived to see it was stacked with work clothes. "Black won't work, I think I need to wear something colorful. Something delightfully southern."

"Delightfully southern?"

"Yeah, you know, something colorful and feminine. But capable." I pulled out my favorite red slacks that hugged my backside like a lover. "How about this with my black silk top? It says capable and strong but feminine, right?"

"Yes. With those insane black stilettos you'll look gorgeous. As always."

I rolled my eyes at my best friend's compliment. "Thanks, but I'm just interested in looking like a good front of house manager." I changed quickly and then dug through the lone box that wasn't sitting inside a storage locker, and found my power stilettos, capable of turning any woman into a superhero. "How do I look?"

"Like the world's best front of house manager?"

My shoulders relaxed at her perfectly placed words. "Thanks. Hair?"

"Keep it down," she said and closed the distance between us, scrunching my natural waves with her fingers. "Perfect."

"If I get this job, you, me and the girls are going out for dinner tonight. On me." I hugged Valona and held her in my arms for a longer than necessary. "Thank you for bringing this up."

"Don't be silly, I've just got you back in town and I'm not ready to lose you to the big city again."

"That's not going to happen. I'm sorry I stayed away for so long and missed so many years with the girls. It feels silly in hindsight, to let him keep me away for so long, but after things fell apart with Dexter, it just brought it all back to the surface."

"It's all right, Pip, I understand. Randy died in the

middle of divorcing me, so trust me when I say that I get the baggage. If not for the girls having a solid community here, I would have gone away too."

I squeezed my best friend a little tighter. "I'm so happy I get to hug you anytime I want now." I pulled back with a smile, kissed Valona's cheek and rushed out the door with my black purse flung over my shoulder, car keys fisted in my hand. "Wish me luck."

"You won't need it," she called after me and I let those four words boost my confidence as I took the short drive to The Old Country House, which was even more gorgeous than the photos, and took the left lane that led to Dark Horse.

I sat in my car for exactly one minute, calming my breaths and giving myself a quick pep talk. "One jerk of a chef in Chicago doesn't define you. You know your stuff and you are an asset to any restaurant smart enough to give you a chance." I let my eyes connect in the mirror and smiled. "You got this."

I rushed inside, lest anyone else show up and try to take the job that was—clearly—meant to be mine.

Less than a minute after I entered, a long and lean man in a three piece navy blue suit with merlot window pane pinstripes strolled out to greet me with a pleasant smile. He looked as if he'd stepped right from the pages of a fashion magazine, which put him dressed even more fancy than me. "Welcome to Dark Horse. What can I do for you today?"

I put on my biggest welcoming smile and held out a hand. "I'm Pippa Carson and I am your new front of house manager."

"I'm Devon," he said with a hint of a smile and motioned me to a booth in the middle of the dining room after I handed him my resume.

I look around the place, excited about making my mark on a brand new restaurant. "The décor is beautiful, a bit rustic, but no doubt this is a fine dining establishment. It has character and that can go along way for helping a new restaurant stand out in a crowd." I was rambling, I felt it down to my core, but I couldn't seem to stop myself. "This place will do good business even without the built-in help from the events taking place on the property."

"Tell me about Chicago." His words were short and to the point, delivered without emotion.

I nodded, feeling my nerves rise as I recounted the events that led to my demise in a clipped, emotionless tone. "The chef, Rodrick, grabbed me by the arm and then squeezed when I told him to let me go. He didn't, so I hit him with the leg of lamb he refused to redo for a paying customer." I shrugged as if getting fired didn't still burn. "The lamb was dry and he wouldn't hear of it, refused to even taste it and instead got physical with me. It wasn't my finest moment, but he's the only temperamental chef to ever get that reaction out of me."

The man, Devon, stared at me for a long time, probably trying to figure out if I was a diva or a crazy person. My hope started to fade the longer the silence persisted, but I kept my spine straight and my shoulders squared, projecting a confidence that dwindled with every passing second.

"Do you consider yourself difficult to work with?"

"No, and I don't think anyone I've worked with in the past, other than Rodrick, would disagree. I pay attention to culinary trends, both in food and décor. I'm great with customers, listening to their needs and cooling tempers without running to the chef constantly or giving away the whole menu for free. I expect a lot from my staff because that's what fine dining requires, but I'm easy to get along with as long as you do your job." I sighed and prepared myself for what he would say next. "I won't let myself be bullied or demeaned, no matter how talented the chef is."

Devon took in my words and nodded before a smile lit up his face turning him from average to good looking. "Excellent to hear. You'll love Chef Nina, she's as quirky as her food, and she's more of a hippie chick than a bully."

I nodded at his words before understanding dawned. "I will? Does that mean that I'm hired?"

"It does. On a ninety day probationary period, of course. Either of us can part ways with in that time for any reason at all. If you make to the ninety-first day, we'll start with a one year contract."

"Oh, wow. Thank you, Devon. I promise I will not let you down." My heart raced inside of my chest like I'd just finished a marathon. This was my second chance, one I desperately needed. "Thank you."

"No thanks necessary. I need a solid house manager, and aside from that one incident, your credentials are good. I'll double check them, obviously, but barring any deviant behavior, you have the job."

I accepted his outstretched hand and shook it with far more enthusiasm than I probably should have. "Do you have a set schedule, or are you a hands-off owner."

"Neither. I'm not the owner, I'm his assistant."

"Oh. You're so well-dressed, like every owner I've ever met." It was like they had to make sure we all knew they wouldn't lower themselves to do anything to help out in the front or back of the house.

"Thanks. I try." Devon sighed and handed me a stack of papers. "The owner will be home in a few days, but you should expect to take the reins around here as we get ready for the Grand Opening."

Take the reins? "Is he, um, does he..." I snapped my mouth shut before I insulted a man I'd never met.

"He is new to this business, this industry, but very eager and determined to make this place a success," Devon supplied helpfully. "When can you start?"

"As soon as you need me." I had a job. Not even twenty-four hours in town and I could tick one item off my to do list. "Is tomorrow too soon?"

"Tomorrow is perfect. Nine o'clock sharp and we can go over everything you'll need to know."

"I'll see you then, Devon. Thank you again. So, so much." He walked me to the door with an amused grin, that didn't offend me in the least. I was happy to have this job, excited that I wouldn't have to start over at the bottom of the ladder. At forty. I practically skipped back to my car with a grin so wide it made my face hurt, and the best part of all? The smile didn't leave for the rest of the day.

For the first time in two months, I could relax. I could breathe again and it wasn't all due to the dewy Tennessee air.

CHAPTER 5
RYAN

It feels good to be home.

That was the main thought that went through my head as I stood in the middle of my living room with the furniture covered and dust everywhere. Despite the fact that it took an extra week longer than planned to get back to Carson Creek, I felt nothing but glad to be home. I surveyed my place and sighed with relief to be in my own place, with my own things.

"Home sweet home."

Never one to dwell on anything, I opened all the windows on the first floor to let the warm breeze through and cranked up the radio while I unpacked my bags and separated them between clothes that went into the laundry and those that went into my closet. The first day after a tour was always busy, because unlike my brothers, I refused to hire a housekeeper into my personal space to put their hands all over my belongings. Besides, hiring a housekeeper in Carson Creek meant hiring one of the older ladies who used to babysit me, or worse, teach me in school.

I was perfectly capable of doing my own laundry, mostly. Sure, every few months I ended up with a few pink shirts that used to be white, but I was a grown man, and I could take care of myself.

Mostly.

"Stupid damn…son of a…gun. Just go where you belong, dammit!"

I froze at the sound of the utterly feminine voice wafting in through my living room windows, and cursing up a storm. Intrigued, I made my way to the corner of the house; where I spotted a denim-clad behind wiggling half in and half out of the house next door.

The house next door.

"Stupid damn thing! Just get the hell in there, would ya!" A low, feminine growl reached me, a sound that hit me right behind the zipper of my well-worn Wranglers.

It would be the neighborly thing to do to go out there and help her. Right? Right. I trotted down the seven steps I hadn't traipsed in too long to remember, jogged across the yard and hopped the fence. With my shoulders squared, I prepared to be the good southern boy I was raised to be, because it was the kind thing to do, and not because she had a sweet voice with that sexy southern twang that's been smoothed away by time away from the deep south.

"Stupid damn thing," she grunted and took a step back to glare at the chair. Hands on her hips, she engaged in a standoff with the inanimate object. Thick red hair tumbled around her shoulders and down her back, but all I could see was her round ass and slim waist. To top it all off, her potty mouth did wicked, wicked things to me. "Idiot."

"Need some help?"

The buxom redhead froze at the sound of my voice and I prepared myself for a roundhouse kick to the head. Or hopefully, a sultry, come hither smile. She turned and I made sure my gaze slid from her tight round butt to her slender waist and a hint of side boob that was more than a handful. A perfect handful.

I should have been paying more attention to my body and less to hers, because my fingers tingled in that telltale way they always did when a certain woman was nearby. The atmosphere was electrified, and I felt my breath catch in my throat before it dropped to my chest.

No, it can't be.

It couldn't be her. Last I heard she was off in the Midwest somewhere catering to people with more money than sense. My eyes narrowed as her profile came into focus. Ski jump nose, check. Full, pouty lips the color of strawberries, check. Smattering of freckles on both cheeks that made her look much younger than she was, but she secretly hated them. *Of course, it's her.*

Pippa turned to face me, big sapphire blue eyes a complete blank as they took me in. Icy as hell, she folded her arms and looked right through me. "Nope. All good, thanks." Dismissing me, she turned away and continued to glare at the chair.

I shouldn't have said anything. I should have just turned away and accepted that she didn't want my help. I should have just left her alone and went back inside. I should have done any one of those things, or all of them, but that just wasn't my style.

"What are you doing here, Pippa?"

She didn't budge, didn't flinch at my words, my tone, or my question. "I could ask you the same question, but I won't. Because I don't care."

"No shit. But I do."

Her delicate shoulders lifted and fell in a nonchalant shrug. "That sounds like a personal problem." Instead of turning to glare at me, to spew some hate my way, she bent over and started to tug on the piece of furniture. Again. It moved an inch, maybe two, but Pippa was too stubborn to ask for help.

"Answer the damn question."

"Go away, Ryan. I'm busy."

"Yeah, busy doin' a whole lot of nothin' from my perspective." I took a few steps forward and pushed

Pippa aside with my hips, giving the flowery chair a good hard tug.

Pippa's small hands landed on my side and shoved, hard enough to make me stumble. "I don't need your help. I can take care of *my place* on my own."

Pippa had always been strong, even stronger than she knew, but she was equally as stubborn, willing to do things the hardest way possible rather than ask for help. "Yeah, I know you can do it on your own, Miss Independent, but with my help you'll be done a lot sooner and cursing a hell of a lot less."

"Don't count on it," she grumbled under her breath. With a determined glint in her eyes, Pippa eyed the offensive thing and let out a frustrated breath before she bent over and tugged it some more.

Nothing happened.

"Offer stands," I told her, not bothering to conceal my amusement.

"Fine. You push and I'll pull." Pippa waved at me, as if I took orders from her.

Not anymore, babe. "I don't think so, sweetheart. You push and *I'll* pull. I've got more muscles and about five inches on you, Squirt." I punctuated the words with a bicep flex and a wink.

Her face turned a deep shade of red at the nickname I'd given her way back before I noticed her lips and her curves, before I knew that her strawberry lips tasted like bubble gum. "Whatever. Let's just get this over with so you can go away."

"Wow, you're welcome." Pippa stared at me with a blank expression. "*Thank you* is customary when someone helps you out."

"Only when that help was requested. You're trespassing, I could have shot you. Could have smashed your head with that shovel over there, and walked away without repercussions. I didn't, so let's consider that a win for you."

Ouch. Still mad, I guess. "Push on three," I told her instead of engaging her in an argument destined to become a fight.

The silence was tense as we moved the chair down the deck steps and to the concrete slab covered with a rainbow sun umbrella. Ten minutes later and a few beads of sweat, and we were done.

"Thanks," Pippa muttered reluctantly in her haughtiest voice before she folded her arms expectantly, and waited for my retreat. "Goodbye."

I hated that word. It was so final, the way she said that word. The same way she'd whispered it to me, with tears in her eyes, more than twenty years ago. "Pippa." Too much time had passed, too many years of silence and avoidance. It was time to fix things between us.

"Goodbye, Ryan."

"Pippa, come on. We're going to be neighbors for at least the next few months, depending on your plans."

"My plans are none of your business. You made sure of that."

As if I could forget. "But we're neighbors."

She shook her head and flicked those sexy waves off her shoulders. "No. We are just two people who live next door to one another. There's no reason we need to talk or engage at all. We're strangers now, and I think we should just keep it that way."

"I disagree."

Pippa folded her arms, a defensive gesture if I ever saw one, and raised her chin high in the air. "Good thing it isn't up to you, then." The look of steely determination in her deep blue eyes sucked me in even as everything about her screamed that she wanted me anywhere but in her backyard. In her life. "Just leave, Ryan. You did it once without a backwards glance, should be easier this time since we're nothing to each other."

Nothing. In her eyes we were nothing more than two people who used to know each other, who used to mean something to one another. We were less than strangers. We were, in her words, nothing. "That's a damn lie and you know it." I made the biggest mistake of my life with this woman, and two decades later, she still couldn't forgive me.

"I know what happened and what didn't. You can rewrite history if you want, so assuage your own guilt, but I want no part of it. Now, get the hell off my property."

I nodded and let a slow grin spread across my face. "I'll go, Pippa. For now, I'll go. But I'm gonna be around for a good long while, and I plan to make things right, whether you like it or not."

"There is no way you can make things right, Ryan. So just go back to your house and your life, and do what you've done for the past twenty years. Pretend I don't exist." With an annoyed grunt and a roll of her eyes, Pippa stormed off inside the house and slammed the door hard enough to rattle the windows.

Message received.

But now I had another distraction.

Plotting ways to get Pippa to forgive me.

CHAPTER 6
PIPPA

"At first I thought I was hallucinating, maybe having one of those walking nightmares, or just imagining things. I figured that being back here was messing with my head.

But nope, it was him. Ryan Gregory right there in my yard. My new neighbor." My dumb damn luck. And it wasn't just Ryan Gregory, forty year old aging rocker. No, that would have been easier than Ryan *I-haven't-aged-in-twenty-years* Gregory with his sparkling hazel eyes that shone green and gold in the sunshine, and his fitted jeans hanging low on his waist. T-shirt clinging to all the right places. "Not a damn beer belly in sight."

Valona let out a loud belly laugh and shook her head. "He does live here, which you'd know if you ever came home for more than a few days at a time."

She was right, but life wasn't quite that simple. "It's

not like you can leave a restaurant for weeks on end, Val."

"Maybe so, but your method of absolute avoidance has officially bitten you in the behind. What are you going to do?"

"What am I going to do?" As if there was *anything* to do. "I'm going to do nothing, because there is nothing to be done. He's my neighbor and I hate it, but I have a job and a place to live so I'm happy. Satisfied." And if I could arrange my schedule just so, I could avoid seeing him altogether.

Surprise flashed in Valona's eyes but she said nothing, just flashed a tight smile and shook her head as if I was the one being ridiculous. "How good did he look?"

I shrugged. "He looked all right." As gorgeous as he ever was. No, he was even better than he'd been as a twenty year old wannabe rock star. Those intervening years had been kind to him. Ryan had the kind of wear and tear that a certain type of man—rugged and low maintenance—wore well. Extremely well. Women of a certain age probably found him completely and totally irresistible. Not me. Definitely not me.

But...some women. Somewhere out there in the world.

Valona tossed her head back and laughed. "You are so full of it, Pippa. I saw him when he was here a few months back and the man is even more gorgeous than when he was a boy. That whole soulful, rugged rocker thing looks good on him, and you damn well know it."

"If that's the kind of thing you go for, sure he looks good. I prefer my men a little more clean-cut these days." Men who saw a barber regularly were stable men, reliable men. The kind of man who wouldn't just upend your future plans to chase his dreams. And not even bother to ask you to come with him.

Valona's laughter faded and she let out a contemplative sigh. "Randy was as clean-cut as they come, not even a five o'clock shadow to speak of, and he came home every night from work to have dinner with me and the girls. He wore a suit and tie even on the weekends, but he was still planning to rip my heart out. To walk away without a backwards glance, Pippa."

Shit. "I'm sorry, Val. I didn't mean to bring up bad memories."

She waved away my concern the way she always did. "It's not bad, not anymore. It just really pisses me off that I didn't find out until after he was already dead, because then I couldn't be angry with him; couldn't confront him about the fact that he'd said nothing about being unhappy or in love with someone else. He took away my anger and forced me to play the grieving widow because that's what Belle and Bridget needed from me."

"Yeah," I sighed. "He was a real dirtbag for that." It

made me mad on her behalf. "I can stop at the cemetery and spit on his grave if you want?"

"Don't bother. Once a month I send red and purple Dahlia's to his headstone."

My eyes widened at my so-called sweet friend. "Wasn't he allergic?"

She nodded with an evil grin. "May he sneeze and suffer in peace."

We shared a long laugh, complete with watery eyes and aching sides. "I've missed this. I'm glad to be back."

"Are you?"

I knew she asked because I steadfastly avoided my hometown as much as I could help it. "I am. I love being able to have coffee with you and spending time with you and the girls, invigorates me. I'm sorry I stayed away so long." I had a feeling if I'd been closer I might have noticed a change in Randy's behavior sooner. Val was too busy with the twins to notice much.

"You did what you had to do and I've told you a thousand times, I understand. You came when I needed you."

"Hey, look on the bright side, at least Randy died before he could nickel and dime you out of what you rightly deserve. And best of all? His little slut got nothing." That was the real silver lining in all of this, that the little homewrecker in search of a sugar daddy had to start over with someone else.

Valona let out a shocked gasp that quickly turned to

a laugh. "I can't believe you said that, but I am so glad you did."

"Right?" I held up my coffee mug and clinked it with hers. "To getting the last laugh."

"To finding your passion and putting the past behind you." Valona laughed when I quirked a brow at her. "You'll have to do it sooner or later."

"Later," I said quickly. "I choose later."

"We'll see," she said cryptically and took a long sip of her black coffee loaded with brown sugar. "Tell me about the new job. How's it going? Do you love it? Does the chef really have purple hair?"

Finally something that didn't hurt or annoy me to talk about. I felt my whole body grow lighter as I told Val about working at Dark Horse. "It's great. I love it. The staff is friendly and the atmosphere is chaotic, but not toxic. And yes, Nina does have purple hair. Actually you'll meet her soon. We need publicity shots for the website, and I happen to be best friends with a very talented photographer."

"I don't do headshots, Pippa." The worry in her eyes only confirmed that this was the right decision.

"I don't want headshots, which you could absolutely do. I want candid shots of Nina in the kitchen, giving orders to the staff, maybe even putting the finishing touches on a dish. And the sous chef who just arrived in town two days ago from Greece."

"And you?"

I shook my head. "Not until the probationary period is over. For now I'm just a ghost who helps keep the place running smoothly." I had no doubt that I would get that one year contract and then a three year one after that, but until it was official, I was just a temporary worker.

"So I'm guessing you haven't met the owner yet?"

I ignored the gleam in her eyes. "Nope. He's been out of town on business, but I'll meet him on Friday for Opening Night. You and the girls will be there, right? I've already reserved a table for you."

"Oh I wouldn't miss it for the world."

Her tone, her glee put me on edge, and I couldn't say why. "Really?"

"A chance to dress up and have someone else cook a meal? Absolutely."

Oh. Right. "Perfect. I gotta run, but thanks for the coffee. Yours always tastes so much better than mine."

"Fresh beans," she said and walked me to the door. "Have a good day at work."

"You too. You're doing graduation photos for some of the high school seniors, right?"

"Yes. It's not what I hoped to be doing, but the parents are willing to pay my fee to have professional photos to commemorate the milestone, so I'm going to slap on a smile and make it happen."

"Just remember that jobs like this will give you more time and freedom to photograph what you're passionate about." I pulled Valona in for a hug and jogged down the stairs towards my car. "I hear the Virginia Bluebells are starting to bloom, if you're in need of a non-human subject to photograph."

Valona's eyes widened and I could see the wheels turning as I slid behind the wheel, waved goodbye and made my way to Dark Horse. The next few days would be busy leading into Opening Night, and I planned to make sure it was a roaring success.

CHAPTER 7
RYAN

"I was beginning to wonder if you were ever going to set foot in this place again." Devon greeted me at the Dark Horse entrance with a smile.

"I didn't want to get in the way of all the preparations for tonight." The truth was, I didn't want to distract the new manager. Not that I was some egotistical rock star, but I knew that some people found it difficult to act normal in front of famous people. "How are things going?"

"Excellent!" Devon waved me in with a curious look. "Are you all right, Boss?"

"I'm fine. Just a little out of sorts, I guess." Most of it had to do with a curvy little redhead who wouldn't give me the time of day. Where Pippa went every day for ten hours or more, I hadn't a damn clue, but she left early and came home late, as if she was avoiding me. "The invitation was a nice touch." I held out the black paper Stetson with the gold script on the front and back. "How much will they set me back?"

"Under budget," Devon assured me. "The manager used one of those craft websites with competitive prices and a free promo." He turned the invitation over and pointed to the bottom where in small script were the words Crafts by Elinore. "They went out to the whole town and then some."

"And then some?" Dark Horse was a local restaurant in a small town. "Why?"

"We're just a stone's throw from Nashville and it's a great enticement for city folk to choose Carson Creek over all the other small towns in the area with B&B's and beautiful scenery."

I frowned at Devon. "According to the manager?"

"Yep. She knows her stuff, and best of all, she knows the area. You'll like her," he assured me with a clap on the back. "Kitchen first?"

I nodded and followed Devon through the swinging wooden doors that separated the kitchen from the dining room. I'd come in a few hours before the grand opening officially started to get staff introductions out of the way so that everyone can be free of interruptions when things really got underway. And to see what my money was paying for.

The kitchen was a madhouse. It felt like there were a

hundred people in white busy prepping, but it couldn't be more than a dozen. Running around, chopping, barking orders and laughing, almost choregraphed as they worked together. How anyone could work in this noise was beyond me, but I kept that thought to myself.

"Attention kitchen staff." Devon barely raised his voice over the noise but somehow they all stopped and turned towards the door. Towards us. "This is Ryan Gregory. Yes, *that* Ryan Gregory, but he's also the owner of this place."

"Holy fuck sticks, you're actually Ryan Gregory." A woman with purple hair took a few steps forward with a wide grin as she extended her hand. "I'm Chef Nina and dammit man, I am huge fan. *Hate To See You Go* is one of my all-time favorites. Nice to meet you." She was a fan, clearly, but not starstruck, and I liked her right away.

"Nice to meet you too. It's always nice to meet a fan, even more when she's a talented chef. You have everything you need for tonight?"

"Oh yeah. Devon said you'd be coming in today, so I have samples of everything for you when you're ready."

I blinked and turned to Devon. "Seriously?"

"Yep."

I turned back to Nina with a smile. "That would be great. Just give me twenty minutes and I'll be ready."

Nina nodded and went back to the sizzling flat top grill, giving me a chance to meet and greet the rest of the kitchen staff; they all looked to be born within the last twenty years. Each and every one of them looked like they belonged backstage with their tattoos and piercings, and intricate hair. Devon said they were capable, and that's all I really cared about.

"Ready to meet the manager?"

I nodded and followed Devon back to the dining room. "Did you pick infants to make me feel old?"

Devon barked out a laugh that echoed in the dining room as he led me down a dimly lit hall that led to the manager's office. "Nah, that was just an added bonus."

"You sure they're all qualified?"

"I'm certain. Talented kitchen staff will go wherever there's a chance for them to stand out or work with a talented chef like Nina."

"Thanks for not telling them who the owner was." The last thing I needed was super fans and groupies on my payroll.

"I wanted people who actually know how to work in a kitchen and a dining room, not people trying to bang the boss."

I clapped him on the back in appreciation with a grin. "And that's why you're my go-to guy."

"That, and you don't have the patience for the details."

"True," I agreed. "Anything I need to know about the manager?"

"Not much. She's a little high strung, but damn is she capable. Saved you a good chunk of change on stock, and made some deal with two local farmers to give Nina first choice on produce and meat. And we got an exclusive on a few local wines and beers for the first month of business. You'll like her."

His words intrigued me. "Let's meet her, then."

Devon knocked on the door and pushed it open at muffled words that could have been "come in" or "go the hell away" but he seemed to understand perfectly. He motioned me in and I stepped inside...into an empty office.

"Just a sec." The muffled feminine voice was slightly familiar, but that could have been my imagination. "Got you, little sucker!" A crop of tussled red waves appeared first, and then an all-too familiar face with a familiar smile that I hadn't been privy to in twenty years. "Devon, my friend, stop plugging your devices straight into the wall. It's a recipe for disaster."

Devon grinned, his cheeks turning a light shade of pink at her smile. "Right. I'll do my best to remember. Again."

Pippa stood and swiped her hands on the side of her black slacks with a sigh. "I've added surge protectors, so now you have no choice." Finally, she realized there was someone else in the room and when Pippa realized *who* that someone was, her smile faded. "What are you doing in here?"

I stared at Pippa in her black slacks and paper-thin silky white blouse that showed off the outline of her bra, the peaks of her nipples and the swell of her gorgeous tits, and felt my body answer in response. She was even more gorgeous now than she'd been as a girl on the cusp of womanhood. Her angry expression shouldn't have made me smile, but it did. Something about an angry redhead, no, there was something about *this* particular angry redhead that instantly infused my body with heat. I turned to Devon with a wicked grin.

"You want to tell her, or should I?"

Devon realized too late, that maybe he should have shared the owner's identity with the front of house manager. "Oh, um, Pippa, this is Ryan, whom you already seem to know."

"Yeah," she growled. "I do."

"Ryan owns Dark Horse."

Her gaze narrowed, her lush pink lips tightened into a straight white line, and her shoulders fell in either resignation, or disappointment, I couldn't tell for sure. "You? You're the owner."

"I am."

The look of utter devastation on her face was like a knife straight to my gut, but this wasn't the emotional girl of eighteen who wore her heart on her sleeve. This version of Pippa was older and wiser, and sure, a little bit harder.

"Am I missing something?" Devon sounded concerned, like his big plan for a smooth opening was about to go up in smoke.

Pippa shook her head as a low, almost silent breath fell from her lips. "Nope, nothing at all. Ryan and I used to know each other about a million years ago, that's all." She refused to look in my direction as she ran her fingers through thick waves and gave a curt nod to Devon. "I'm going to go make sure everything is perfect and let you guys talk. If you need anything, I'm around." Pippa skirted around the desk, taking the longer route around Devon to avoid being anywhere near me.

"We should talk." The words were out of my mouth before I thought better about it. Devon held his breath as Pippa turned slowly, her gaze met mine reluctantly.

"Am I fired?"

What? Did she really think I would fire her just like that? "No, of course not."

"All right." Delicate shoulders fell another inch in relief but she was still wound as tight as a screw. "I need to make sure the wine is chilled and that the waitstaff has all the last minute menu changes, and I'll return shortly."

Her agreement, reluctant though it was, buoyed me. As the owner, she couldn't ignore me the way she could as a neighbor, but still it felt like a good sign. She hadn't quit or stormed off, which meant she wanted to be here. I could work with that.

"Okay."

Still, she hurried out of the office as if she couldn't wait to get away from me.

After a long silence, Devon cleared his throat. "Something you want to tell me?"

"Yeah. Pippa is the one who got away." Ran away was more accurate. She'd run like the hounds of hell were nipping at her backside, and I was the reason for it. Now she was back and working for me.

"She's *Hate To See You Go*?"

I nodded. "Yep."

"*The Hauntress*?"

"Her, again."

Devon blinked. "*Outside Your Bedroom Window*?"

I glared at him. "You gonna go through my whole damn discography? Let me save you a few breaths, Devon. Yeah that's her. She's the one they're all about. Every last one of 'em."

"Wow," he sighed. "That's one hell of a coincidence."

"No kidding." What were the odds that the woman I let slip through my fingers would eventually return home and work for the side project that was meant to distract me from a life half-lived?

Devon chuckled and shook his head. "I'm happy I'll be sticking around for a while. This is going to be interesting."

Pippa sat across from me at the four-top table where Nina had set up the menu samples for me, and blew out a breath. "We have about fifteen minutes to *talk,* and then five minutes to get ready for customers. So, you're the owner."

"I am." I wanted to tell her everything, about how I was feeling out of sorts about where my life was headed outside of my career. I wanted to tell her that this was something just for me, to distract me from all the things I didn't have that a man of forty should have. A wife and kids. A picket fence and a pet. Family vacations. A full life.

"Why a restaurant?"

I shrugged at the surprising question. "My business manager thought a fine dining place could do well in this town."

I could tell my answer disappointed her but I didn't know why. "I've been working in this industry for a while now, so if you have questions, I'm sure I can answer them."

Ah, so we were keeping this professional, then? I would allow it. For now. "Great because I feel out of my depth, but Devon has done nothing but sing your praises."

She nodded absently. "He's goal oriented and efficient, which I appreciate."

"What happened to Chicago?"

Pippa shrugged. "Chicago is over. I'm here now." A wave of sadness washed over her but disappeared just as quickly. She visibly shook off her emotions as if remembering who she was talking to. "Are you up for some interviews tonight? Seven journalists were sent invites and five confirmed, and they'll definitely want to talk to Ryan Gregory."

"At least someone does," I growled under my breath, frustrated that Pippa was so closed off when she used to be so open with her emotions.

She let out a frustrated sigh, but that was the only hint that she was unhappy about this little chat. "Plenty of people will want to talk to you tonight. I assume you're more comfortable speaking in public these days?"

My lips curled into a smile at her reminder. "Not so much. Usually Derek and Roman are happy to answer questions and smile for the camera."

Pippa nodded, but there was no smile at the memories of how I used to tremble in fear at the idea of speaking in public. All I ever wanted to do was sing. "Luckily, you know most of these people so it should be easy enough to chat a little, to welcome them to your restaurant."

"Feel free to have some," I told her and motioned to the small plates scattered around the table.

"No thanks, I sampled the menu earlier this week," she said absently and pulled a sheet of paper from her leather folder. "I created a list of things you might want to mention, especially when you talk to the press." She handed me a sheet filled with about a dozen bullet points.

"What's all this?" It looked to me exactly what I hated about dealing with the press, the whole interaction was so forced. So phony. "I don't do talking points."

Pippa's nostrils flashed briefly before she banked her emotions once again with the help of a long sigh. "Consider them points of gratitude, then, for the invitation designer, the local brewers and vintners who were eager to help out another local business owned by a local." When I said nothing, she sighed again and tapped the paper. "Be sure to mention that you and Margot attended school together, and that this venue space will invigorate the local economy, which means a lot to you since this town gave you your start."

I blinked up at her, brows dipped in confusion. "You said you didn't know I was the owner."

"I didn't. I had a rough draft completed and edited it once I found out who the owner was."

"Wow," I sighed in awe. "You *are* good."

Pippa nodded, but said nothing in response to my compliment. "Just be sure to remember the names of the businesses and people. You'll look like you're too good for this place if you have to refer to notes."

Her words burned. "I don't think I'm too good for this place. This is my home. One I returned to often." It was an unnecessary dig, I knew that, but dammit I wanted to get a rise out of this woman.

She ignored the barb directed at her. "I said you'll look that way. You know how the press can be, and I want nothing but positive stories about tonight." Pippa stood and tapped the bottom of the page. "Use these hashtags when you post on social media tonight."

I blinked. "Social media?"

"Yes, to generate a buzz about Ryan Gregory's new restaurant venture. The one he generously partnered with his hometown buddies to keep this town just as it is. Perfect."

Damn, she's still as fiery as she is gorgeous.

"Got it?"

I nodded, but Pippa missed it since her gaze was on her phone. "Yeah, I think so."

"Good. Enjoy the food. Nina is an excellent chef. The doors open in eight minutes. Good luck tonight."

I watched Pippa walk away, knowing I had a hell of a lot to make up for, but I had no clue where to begin.

CHAPTER 8
PIPPA

It was only thirty minutes into Opening Night, but so far it was going well. I managed to shrug off the conversation with Ryan and focus on greeting the guests, giving them a quick rundown of the local ingredients as well as the dishes I found delicious from my earlier tasting. I am the epitome of a calm and cool professional throughout the night, ignoring the inner turmoil caused by finding out Ryan was my new boss. And our brief conversation.

Inner turmoil?

I sounded like an idiot, because there shouldn't be any turmoil. I was a forty year old woman and high school was—literally—a lifetime ago. It didn't matter that no man I ever dated, or married, ever stacked up, ever made me feel even a fraction of what Ryan had made me feel. Maybe that was the nature of first loves. And first heartaches.

The men who had come after Ryan, it wasn't their fault, not completely. They got a different version of me, a woman who didn't trust easily, who got out before a man had a chance to leave her. A short-lived marriage had taught me that even though I'd moved on from Ryan, his betrayal had fundamentally changed me, altered my ability to trust. To stick.

I shook off all thoughts of Ryan and the past and smiled down at the couple with matching silver curls. "Your server will be with you shortly."

"Pippa, do you have a minute? I have a few questions for you." Ryan's smooth voice startled me but I recovered quickly, turning to him with a mischievous smile.

"Mr. Gregory, have you met Celia and Donovan Markson?"

He blinked, surprised and shook his head. "I don't think I've had the pleasure. You folks local?"

Celia nodded. "For the past two years, ever since we retired in fact."

"Well I hope you folks enjoy Carson Creek as much as I have over the years." He was *on,* in celebrity mode, and I just watched in awe. He was so smooth, so easy with complete strangers. Unlike the boy who had panic attacks before every performance. "Pippa?"

I nodded and followed Ryan down the hall, ignoring the way his well-worn jeans hugged his ass and gripped his thighs, because he was my boss. *Only* my boss. I stepped inside the office behind him, keeping the desk and then some between us.

"What can I do for you Mr. Gregory?"

He let out a loud, full-throated laugh and shook his head. "Mr. Gregory? Pippa I've known you since you were knee high to a grasshopper, I know what you taste like, you're going to *Mister* Gregory me?"

I nodded defiantly. "Yes. You are my boss, and that's the appropriate way to address you," I informed him in my haughtiest tone, the one I used with unruly customers who tried to get free food by lying about being unsatisfied or worse, having hair in their food. "We *knew* each other, way back in the day. We haven't known each other for more than twenty years and I think it's best if we keep it professional."

"I don't think that's best at all, Pippa."

I sighed and tried to push down my annoyance. It wouldn't do any good to get fired on opening night. I needed this job as much as I wanted it, even if it meant dealing with Ryan.

"You said you had some questions for me?"

"I do. Are you married?"

Seriously? "No."

His smile was tight. "Ever been married?"

"Is this really what you interrupted me to ask, Ryan, *Mr. Gregory*?"

He smirked as if that slip was some kind of victory.

"Maybe I'm just trying to break the ice so we can have a civil conversation. Have you ever been married?"

I could keep arguing and let his scent, leather and pine and sandalwood, invade my senses, or I could just answer his absurd questions. "Once for about sixteen months." It wasn't a bad marriage, we just weren't compatible.

"Me too," Ryan sighed. Was that relief? I couldn't be sure, and I didn't dare ask. "Mine lasted a little more than two years, probably because I was on the road for much of that time."

I stared at Ryan, my expression blank even as my heart drummed against my chest bone at the thought that he'd met someone else, fallen for her and loved her enough to marry her. To give her his name, while he'd been happy to walk away from me.

"Kids?"

"Nope."

"Me neither." His spoke the words easily enough, but that bittersweet look on his face told me he regretted that fact. I hated that I could still read him so well. "Are we going to be friends Pippa?"

"No Ryan, we aren't." I shook my head and stood a little taller, reaching for all the confidence I could muster in the face of his too-serious stare. "You own this restaurant and I manage it. You're my boss and I think that's plenty." I thought it was too much actually, but I liked this job and it allowed me to re-settle in my hometown. I would play as nice as I could.

"Right, but we're also neighbors. Avoiding one another isn't really an option."

Wanna bet? "We're neighbors, *for now*. This place and this town isn't your full-time reality, Mr. Gregory."

"I'll be home for the next three months, possibly six. I haven't even starting writing our next album yet, so I'll be around for...a while."

Dang it! "My job is stationary, so unless I need to start job hunting again, I'm not going anywhere."

He flashed a victorious grin as if he had anything to do with my answer and then Ryan stood a little taller. "Then we have time to get to know each other again. To become friends once again."

"That's not going to happen."

His brows dipped into a frown that I used to know well. "And why the hell not?" His rangy muscular arms folded across his chest, his stare expectant. "Well?"

"You really want to know?"

"I'm asking, aren't I?" He wasn't just asking, though. He was also demanding an answer. Demanding the truth.

"Because I don't spend time with people I don't trust, and I don't trust you." I'm sure there was a kinder way to say that, but I hadn't planned on saying anything at all until he pressed the issue.

His expression turned dark as if he was the offended party. "I never lied to you."

"Maybe not, but you led me to believe a lie which is pretty much the same thing. So let's just keep our relationship strictly professional."

"I'm sorry, Pippa. I can't do that."

Thankfully someone knocked on the door, and I turned around in a flash, a wide grin pasted on my face as one of the waitresses appeared, trying hard to look as if she hadn't heard at least some of our conversation. "I'm sorry to interrupt, but Pippa, I just need a quick refresher on that IPA. It just tastes like soap to me and I don't think that's a selling point."

"No problem, Krista." I flashed a grateful smile to her before turning to Ryan. "Gotta go, Mr. Gregory. Tonight is a big night for this place. And for you."

His gaze seared through me as if he were trying to see past my eyes, past the strong exterior I was determined to present to him and the rest of the world. "We'll continue this discussion at another time, Ms. Carson."

"That won't be necessary," I assure him and turned away quickly to give Krista another quick tutorial before the dining room was flooded with customers.

It didn't take much time before the place was packed. Margot had shown up with a bunch of well-dressed people and taken over a large table in the back of the restaurant. My brother Chase showed up, alone of course, and I hugged him tight, smiling as if we hadn't seen each other in ages, when I'd seen him just a few days ago. "Thanks for coming."

Chase shrugged off my words with a smile and a hint of a blush. "My sister is in charge of the biggest restaurant opening in town. Where else would I be?"

"Good answer. No date?"

He quirked a brow in my direction as if to say, *Really?* "How are things working out with the boss?"

I rolled my eyes in response. "Things are...working out." That was as much as I was prepared to say—to anyone—about learning that my new boss was the former love of my life.

"Right. Can I get a table?"

"For one?" It was the perfect opening to find out if my brother was dating since he kept his own counsel, which I supposed was a way to keep his private life, well private.

"That would be great, actually."

My shoulder sank. "It really wouldn't be, Chase. Not tonight. You're the mayor and you should be mingling. Want me to see if there's room at Margot's table for you?"

"God, no! The last thing I want is to talk business tonight." His eyes bounced around the dining room in search of a table to crash. "I'm sure someone will let me join them."

"Hi, Mayor Chase!" Belle stopped beside me and

stared up at my brother with a beauty queen smile. "You can sit with us, can't he Mom?"

Valona and Bridget joined us a few moments behind the exuberant Belle. "If Chase doesn't mind eating with three chatty females, he's more than happy to join us for dinner."

My brother looked at the pre-teens and grinned. "You girls are twelve, right?" They both nodded. "You promise not to talk about the stock market and ways to turn Main Street green?"

Bridget giggled and nodded her agreement. "Not a problem at all."

Belle shrugged. "Solar panels are a cheaper way to light the streets at night, but fine, I promise." She rolled her eyes with an exacerbated sigh that had all the adults smiling.

"Right this way," I told the now table of four because unlike many restaurant managers, I didn't mind pitching in to help out the hostess when things got busy. Before she could sit, I grabbed my best friend by the arm and pulled her a few steps back. "You could have told me that Ryan owns this place, Val."

"I tried, but you were too gung ho to change your life, to land that job, to listen. I seem to remember trying to tell you a few times." Valona wasn't affected at all by my angry tone.

"You had days since then to say something. Anything, Val." I hated that he'd blindsided me. Twice.

"I could have," she conceded with a slightly sympathetic smile. "But that crinkle in your brow is back and so darn amusing."

"Gee thanks," I murmured and swatted her hand away from said crinkle in the middle of my face. "Pretend I've just flipped you the bird, would ya?"

"Nah. This is going to be interesting to say the least, and I could really use some interesting in my life right now."

"Make your own," I growled and pushed her towards the empty space beside Belle.

"But living vicariously through your interesting life is very low stakes for me," she whispered with a giggle.

"Really making me glad to be home," I told her sarcastically before turning my attention to her daughters. "Don't you girls look pretty today."

"We look the same except for our clothes, Aunt Pippa." Belle's monotone told me exactly what she thought of my compliment.

"Thank you, Aunt Pippa. It's the new lip gloss, cherry shine." Bridget smacked her lips dramatically before a slow smile spread across her face. "Do I look like a teenager?"

"Unfortunately for your mother, you absolutely do."

Her face brightened beautifully. "Thanks." She blushed prettily and I couldn't help but laugh.

"Enjoy the meal guys and I'll try to swing back around in a little bit."

"Good luck," Valona offered.

"Knock 'em dead," Chase encouraged with a wink.

"Have a good night," the twins sing-song shouted in unison.

I looked at the table filled with the people I held closest to my heart. "Have I told you guys how much I love you all? Because I totally do." And with those words, I was off, smiling and laughing and chatting with every person who stepped through the Dark Horse doors.

By the time I locked those doors, my cheeks ached from smiling, my throat was scratchy and my feet were so sore I could no longer feel my toes.

It was a great night.

CHAPTER 9
RYAN

I should have left well enough alone. I should have taken one look at Pippa relaxing in her backyard, low bluesy rock music playing from somewhere I couldn't see, ass wrapped in fringed denim with miles upon miles of long legs on display. Her feet were bare and propped up on a glass table, crossed at the ankles, beside them a distinctive bottle of Tennessee Whiskey and a crystal glass that was too small to be a tumbler and too big to be a shot glass. One of those colorful flowing tops hung off one shoulder, giving her a sexy, breezy bohemian appeal that made a man act contrary to his own best advice.

Don't do it!

That's what my brain shouted at me, what it urged me to do. Stay on my side of the fence and let Pippa enjoy her evening and her whiskey without intrusion. But my heart told me that she looked lonely, that the soft music and her closed eyes were a sign that she was hurting, that she was in need of a friend.

So what did I do? I ignored good sense and trotted down my back steps and hopped the fence separating us with ease, strolling across her expansive green yard with a calm smile, never mind the way my heart pitter-pattered in my chest. Pippa didn't hear me approaching, and I took advantage of her lack of awareness by taking in the vision she made, relaxed and seemingly happy, her lips curved into the barest hint of a smile.

"Want some company?"

She didn't gasp, didn't startle, didn't even open her eyes. The only thing that moved was her lush pink lips. "Nope."

"Really? 'Cause that looks like entirely too much whiskey for an itty bitty thing like you." Goading Pippa wasn't smart. I knew that from past experience, but she couldn't possibly hate me any more than she already did, so I figured it was worth the risk.

She opened her blue eyes. "I'm not a rock star, which means I drink in moderation. Just because the bottle is full doesn't mean I need to empty it tonight."

"Ouch." I rubbed circles in my chest for emphasis. "Your tongue is sharp."

"And my memory long." She tapped her head with a

small quirk of her eyebrow, the one with the tiny scar in it from a drunken mishap down at Starlight Lake. "Take your swagger, your smile and your charm back over that fence, and enjoy a night of solitude. Or not. Just remove yourself from my property."

"I will. I promise." But there was no way in hell I could leave now, with her smelling like vanilla and flowers, and her smooth skin on wicked display. "But first, let's have a drink. For old time's sake."

"No thanks. How about we go our separate ways, for old time's sake? That seems to be more your speed."

"Damn woman, put those claws away."

"Can't," she cooed. "They're for self-protection."

I dropped down in the seat closest to her and let out a long, exhausted sigh. "You don't need to protect yourself from me, Pip."

She winced at my use of her old nickname and pushed herself upright on the cushion covered metal chair. "Yeah, I thought that once too. Turns out, I was wrong."

"So you're ready to talk about this? Us and our past?"

"No. Hell no." She shook her head and kept shaking it as she poured another glass of whiskey and knocked it back in one shot. "There's nothing to talk about. The past is the past. I've learned from it, from you, and I have moved on, Ryan."

"Back to Ryan now, are we?"

"I'm off the clock and you're not my boss at the moment, you're a trespasser." Her big blue eyes weren't wary or weary, they were crystal clear and sober as a priest. "There's nothing for us to talk about."

"I disagree."

Pippa nodded, a smile that wasn't really a smile spread across her face. "Disagree all you want, just have this damn conversation with yourself."

"I have, at least a million times. Never goes the way I want it to."

She huffed, and it could have been a laugh or a snort. "Then maybe it's a conversation you should stop having. There are no answers, no do overs. Nothing said now can change what happened back then."

"It can if we decide it could be." Who in the hell was this stubborn woman who looked and sounded like the reasonable Pippa Carson, always willing to hear someone out, to give them the benefit of the doubt?

You broke her, a voice whispered to me.

"Well it can't."

I reached for the bottle and took a long swig, enough to choke on, but I pushed it down. "You really hate me?"

"Not anymore," she answered honestly. "I spent a lot of time hating you, but it didn't get me anywhere. So I stopped hating you and just accepted the lessons I'd learned."

"The lesson being that you can't trust me?"

"Not just you," she added nonchalantly, as if that wasn't the same thing. Pippa sat up and poured another drink before she shoved the bottle across the table to me. "People tell you all kinds of things, mostly things they think you want to hear. Because it's easier than the truth, easier than saying the hard thing that will certainly hurt you, but that's hard to face head on. So you're left to deal with the truth, the real and unvarnished truth, on your own, and the other person never has to face those consequences."

"You think it wasn't hard on me too?"

She slammed her glass down so hard I though the whole table might shatter. "I don't know Ryan, that's the point. You made your choice, you left without a look back, so you didn't have to face the consequences of anything. It's all in the past now and just because you're back home and bored doesn't mean that I'm ready to excavate the past just to ease your guilt." The words came out on a low, angry growl that was a little sexy too. She stood and yanked the bottle from my hands. "Hop my fence again and you'll find that backside of yours full of buckshot." With those parting words, Pippa marched inside her house, slammed the door at least twice as hard as was required to secure it shut, and locked it up nice and tight for good measure.

I sat out in her yard for a few minutes longer, and her words stuck with me for the entire night. Pippa didn't dislike me, no it was much worse than that. She didn't trust me. Didn't trust anyone, it sounded like, and that was because of me.

I had even more to make up for than I realized. The problem was that the stubborn woman wouldn't even give me the time of day, which meant I had to make her give me time.

CHAPTER 10
PIPPA

"Levi, it's Pippa from Dark Horse." I smiled into the phone at the man's deep voice and seemingly pleased chuckle.

"Pippa, I'd recognize that Tennessee twang with a blend of Chicago accent anywhere." He punctuated the words by making an awful attempt at a so-called Chicago accent. "What can I do for you, ma'am?"

When Levi called me ma'am it didn't make me feel old, and I smiled even wider. "Well, it seems that your amber and pale ales are quite the hit with our customers. Our stock needs to be replenished as soon as you can manage it."

"No kidding?" As a new brewery, Levi & Bros was an unknown entity, and every success came as a shock. "That's great news."

"Excellent news. Congratulations." A figure filled the

doorway of my office and I didn't need to look up to know it was Ryan, but my stupid curious brain looked up the moment his scent reached me. "We have a sort of upscale bachelor party at the end of next week. Steak and beer pairings. Think you can get us some stock by then?"

"Before then, if you like."

I laughed into the phone. "Sooner is always better when it comes to alcohol, I find. As soon as you can get it, we can use it Levi." I motioned for Ryan to step inside, ignoring the way my heartbeat kicked up a notch at the sight of him in loose fitting jeans and a black t-shirt that hugged him everywhere. Everywhere.

"Thank you, Pippa. Since your opening, interest in our beers has doubled. Anything you need, call me."

"You're sweet Levi and one of these days I just might take you up on that offer." He was a sweetheart, even if he was barely thirty years old and a shameless flirt. "I'll send over the order form in just a few minutes."

"I'll keep an eye out. You take care, Pippa."

"Will do." I ended the call and took a look at Ryan, standing in front of my desk with his arms folded, a scowl marring his otherwise handsome face. "What can I do for you, Mr. Gregory?" It was silly, ridiculous even, to keep calling him that, but it got under his skin just enough to make it worth it.

Ryan's nostrils flared at my question, and he shoved his hands deep in his pocket, a telltale sign he was nervous about something. "We have some business to take care of today. Come on."

Immediately I pulled up the restaurant calendar, because I'd have damn well remembered a meeting scheduled with Ryan. "What business? There's nothing on the calendar."

"Calendar?"

I tapped the screen, annoyed. "You know the one where we all know what's going on around here? You have access to it, Devon made sure of it."

Ryan simply stared at me for a long moment, his lips curled into a satisfied smirk. I remembered that look well. "This isn't on the schedule."

Thank goodness. "I can't go anywhere today. Sorry," I told him, not feeling sorry at all.

"The restaurant is closed today."

"Exactly, which is why we have inventory coming in today."

His brows dipped low. "Doesn't Nina handle that?"

"For the food, yes. But there's alcohol coming in, and specialty items for tomorrow's engagement party." Did the man not understand that running a restaurant was a full-time job?

"This will only take a few hours. I promise."

I shook my head, anger warring with disbelief. "I don't have a few hours to spare, Mr. Gregory. We have a lot to do today."

"Devon is on his way in as we speak," he countered

and there went that smug smirk again. "There's a local winery I want to check out, maybe do a deal with them."

"Oh. Well that's great." I sighed and relaxed back in my chair. "You're the boss, so if you like the wine, you're the one with the power to make the deal." This was something that didn't require me to be present. "Good luck."

"I know what kind of wine I like, which is hardly any of 'em. The stuff tastes like vinegar to me, Pippa. But you've worked in restaurants for years, you know what customers like, what's trending and all that. Don't you?" His victorious smile grated on my nerves, but I kept my expression neutral. "Come on, Pip, we'll be gone only a few hours. Tops."

"Fine," I growled just to get this over with. "I need a few minutes and then I'll be ready to go."

"I'm driving," he said and sauntered off.

Two hours later we were still on the road. "Where exactly is this winery?"

A long beat passed before Ryan spoke, giving me time to focus on his strong, calloused hands, handling the steering wheel as if it was his trusted guitar. "Gatlinburg. This winery is doing a lot of eco-growing which apparently changes the taste of the grapes."

"Gatlinburg! That's not a quick day trip like you promised." I shook my head, disgusted that I allowed myself to trust him. Again. "My fault." Anger stewed and I turned my head out the passenger window, barely seeing the beautiful scenery as we zipped past it.

"You're mad."

I snorted at his not-a-question and kept silent. Of course I was mad, he'd interrupted my work day for this, I didn't even know what the hell it was, but it was garbage.

"Pippa." He let out a frustrated sigh. "You're just gonna be silent the entire time? Real mature."

"Not the entire time, just until we get to the winery and I can ask some questions."

"And me?"

"You I have nothing to say to, because you lied to me. Again."

"I did not," he insisted angrily. "This is a day trip and we'll be back in time for you to get some work done."

"Oblivious ass," I muttered more to myself than to Ryan.

"Pardon?" He tugged on his ear as if he didn't hear me and I turned to him with fire in my eyes.

"You heard me you *oblivious ass!* Sure we'll be back before the calendar changes to tomorrow, but it's a four hour drive, plus two or three hours of touring the vineyards, tasting the wines. If we're lucky we might leave for home at six or seven, which puts me back at the restaurant at nine or ten. Does that seem right or fair to you?" He opened his mouth to speak but I plowed straight ahead. "Or it's that it doesn't matter, because you don't have to do the work?" My heart pumped hard as the last few words left my mouth. No one in the world could get to me the way this man could.

"I just want to put the past behind us, Pip. To start over and move forward, maybe even as friends."

Friends? What a joke. "The past *is* behind us. It's history, hell it's ancient history, but that doesn't mean it's forgotten. Why isn't it enough that we can work together and be civil?" That was a challenge all on its own, and it had to be enough. It certainly was enough for me.

"I miss you, Pip."

My heart hitched in my throat at his words. He missed me. What in the hell did that even mean? "You gave me up easily enough, so what's to miss?"

Ryan growled, the sound low and menacing. "I didn't give you up, I went after my dreams Pip. You did the same."

"I could have...whatever." There was no point rehashing a past you couldn't change.

"Now that you're here, that we're both back in town at the same time, I miss you even more than when I was on the road. You're right here, so close, but as far away as if you were still in Chicago. You're here but I can't bask in the glow of your smile. I can't laugh with you, because you don't laugh when I'm around. You don't smile and you don't even seem relaxed, it's like I suck all the joy from your life just by existing."

That was about right. But I wasn't a woman to kick a man when he was down, even if he put himself there. "You no longer have the power to steal my joy, Ryan. If that makes you feel better."

"It doesn't."

"Well I guess you'll have to find a way to make yourself feel better." We made the rest of the drive in silence. No music. No conversation, just one long stretch of silence so loud it was practically a third person in the car with us.

Thankfully, we were both professionals capable of doing the job even through a thick curtain of tension between us. The winery owner and operator received the happy, inquisitive version of us both. "Hello, and welcome to Gatlinburg Wine Commune. I'm Trixie, and this is my life partner, Tucker."

"Nice to meet you," I greeted the couple who looked more like hippie farmers than owners of the fastest growing winery in all of Tennessee. "This place is gorgeous."

"It is, isn't it?" Tucker offered a friendly smile along with a handshake. "Trixie swears the view makes the grapes a little sweeter." He laughed and cast an affectionate look her way and I tamped down the envy. Way down. When was the last time a man looked at me that way?

Long before I was a woman.

The vineyards were so gorgeous they nearly

brought tears to my eyes. Surrounded by vibrant shades of green and the Smoky Mountains in the distance was enough to soothe my frazzled nerves. This place was a perfect spot for a weekend getaway, with or without a man. Every minute we were there, I felt the tension between me and Ryan melt away. Mostly.

"Is it me or is this place like a fairytale?" Ryan's whispered words sent a shiver of awareness through me. He was too close, and he smelled too good.

I nodded and took a few steps away from him. "It's great, it's almost like you can smell the grapes in the air."

Trixie gasped and turned just before we made our way into the wine cellar. "I love that you said that! Every morning I come out and do yoga here because the sweet smell of the grape varietals is the perfect way to start the day."

"Sounds like heaven," I told her honestly.

"You do yoga?" Trixie's question echoed as the door to the cellar opened and Tucker motioned for us to follow him.

"Not since I left Chicago. As soon as I get my schedule to something resembling normal again, I'll start back up." Maybe that's what I needed to get over my anger and inconvenient attraction to the man who—still—stood too close.

"I for one, would love to watch you do yoga in your

backyard." Ryan took advantage of our momentary alone time to...flirt?

"Then I'll make sure to do it indoors."

He laughed, and the sound was rich and smooth, just like the man himself. "Maybe it's time to start my career as a Peeping Tom."

His words teased a reluctant laugh out of me and the answering smile he sent my way nearly stole my breath. "Funny."

"A compliment, even a sarcastic one, I'll take it."

"You've gotten cheesy in your old age."

His bark of laughter was pure amusement, his smile the same boyish grin I fell in love with all those years ago. Before I knew the lies that smile hid. "Maybe just more honest?"

I snorted in disbelief before I could stop myself, thankfully Trixie and Tucker returned just then.

"We'd like to invite you to enjoy our tasting menu so you can see how the wines pair with different cuisines. For this tasting, we serve you a blend of vegan, vegetarian and omnivorous meals so you can make the best recommendations to all of your customers."

"That's brilliant!"

Trixie's approving smile stayed fixed in place throughout the delicious meal that featured cuisines from around the world, and close to a dozen different types of wine.

"Well, what do you think?"

I sat back with a huff and gave my stuffed belly a solid pat. "I think that I'd love to live here forever."

"Friends with good taste are always welcome," Tucker offered with a sincere smile.

"Everything was delicious, without a doubt," I assured him. "But I really loved how each plate highlighted different flavors of the same wines." I turned my attention to Ryan. "What did you think?"

He shrugged and leaned back against the booth seat with a slow grin. "It was all so delicious that I don't know where to begin."

"Start with the wines you liked best."

He nodded and flashed a grateful smile that kicked my heartbeat into overdrive. "The white wines were delicious, pairing with fish and vegetables. Some were sweet and bitter, some had citrus flavors like summertime."

"Every day can be summer with these wines," Tucker answered genuinely.

I nodded. "Perfect for bridal showers, baby showers and brunch."

"We'll just leave you these order forms and give you some time to discuss. We'll be at the bar if you need anything."

Left alone, again, with Ryan, we had no choice now but to talk. "How many white wines do you want to test?"

Ryan nodded and picked up the order form. "I think

a box of each of the ones we like should be perfect for a test run, don't you?"

"This place is close enough that we can place another order quickly if we sell out soon. I think the merlot would be great for the bachelor party coming up."

"Red wine is never difficult to sell, and this stuff is particularly good."

"I agree, and I think the organic labeling will appeal to a younger customer base with money to spend."

Ryan's smile was filled with an emotion that shouldn't be there, shouldn't light his hazel eyes the way they did. "Always with work on your mind, huh?"

"That's why we're here, is it not?"

"Of course, but aren't we just tipsy enough to remember how much we used to like being around one another?"

Yes, absolutely. "No. Not quite that tipsy."

He laughed. "Then let's try a bit more of this Cabernet, I hear it's excellent for relieving anxiety."

"I'm anxiety-free, thank you very much." Still, I accepted the topped up glass with a gentle smile. "You want to talk? Tell me why you opened a restaurant."

My question surprised him, and in true Ryan style, he took his time before answering. "I needed to invest in something, and I wanted something that was just for me. Something that wasn't a Gregory Brothers thing. Does that make sense, or do I sound like a selfish prick?"

"Not selfish, no. You've been living and working and touring with your brothers for plenty of years, Ryan. It doesn't make you selfish to want something that is just for you."

His shoulders relaxed at my words. "Then why do I feel like a traitor?"

"Because you love your brothers, and you feel guilty. I'm guessing they told you that your guilt was unwarranted?" He nodded. "So why do you insist on wallowing in it?"

"Old habit, I guess." Ryan leaned forward and poured more into both glasses. "I want to succeed at something without them. To know that it isn't just the magic of us that caused our success. Roman is going to record a solo album during the break."

"Really? That's exciting. Are you upset?"

"Hell no," he answered quickly and took a few sips from his glass. "I'm proud of him. He wants me to write a few songs for him."

"You're proud of that." It wasn't a question, his chest puffed out a little and his shoulders seemed to expand a little wider as he spoke.

"I am. He asked me because he thinks I'm a great song writer and lyricist. That he recognizes my talent, it means something to me."

Dammit, I didn't want to like Ryan again, and I certainly didn't want to sympathize with him. And I would never, ever reveal that I'd listened to a few of his songs on a loop on and off over the years.

"Congratulations."

"Thanks." A loud crack of thunder tore through the air outside, rumbling the building so hard I thought it might crumble around us. "Sounds like rain."

Thunder and rain in these parts could be nothing, or it could turn into a five-day long storm. "We should get on the road if we're going to get back before the sun comes up."

"No can do, Pip. I need at least," he glanced down at his watch and whistled. "Forty-five minutes before I'm good to drive. This wine has gone straight to my head."

I glared at him. Hard. "I'm fine to drive."

His brows dipped low. "You can drive a manual these days?"

No. "Some."

"Not good enough, sweetheart. No one drives my truck but me, especially someone who can't handle a stick shift."

I wanted to call him every name in the book but I was an adult now, a grown woman capable of keeping her emotions in check. "Fine."

Like she had some kind of radar, Trixie appeared, looking unconcerned about the weather raging around the vineyard. "There's a motel a few miles away if you prefer, but we do have rooms available. We offer them up for all kinds of events."

"That won't be necessary," I assured her. "As soon as the rain lets up and Ryan is okay to drive, we're going to make our way back home." As if the universe had the cruelest sense of humor, a flash of lightning lit up the dining room, another loud roar of thunder sounded, and then the sky opened up. The downpour crashed down against the ceiling and the windows on all sides.

"Could be a few hours," Tucker offered. "You're welcome to wait it out here, but the dining room closes at nine."

I could feel Ryan's smile before I looked across the table at him, all smug and satisfied like he'd won some prize. "Let's just stay here, Pippa."

As if the world was on his side, because of course it was, the rain intensified impossibly. "Looks like we're staying here for the night."

Tucker nodded. "Trixie will show you to the reception area."

"Thank you," I offered with a grateful smile even though grateful was the last thing I was feeling at the moment.

More like railroaded by Mother Nature and Ryan Gregory.

CHAPTER 11
RYAN

"Two rooms, please." Pippa smiled at the young receptionist, jaw clenched as if she could feel my gaze on her.

After a few seconds of typing, she frowned. "I'm sorry ma'am, but there's just one room available tonight."

"One room?" Pippa shook her head, brows dipped into a quick frown. "Does it have two beds?"

"Afraid not," she offered with a sympathetic smile. "It's our Lover's Suite, but it comes with a large king sized bed. If that helps."

"It doesn't," she snapped angrily before her shoulders fell. "I'm sorry, I know this isn't your fault, it's just not the news I wanted to hear. How far away is the next lodging area?"

"A few miles, but in this weather, you should call

before leaving. It's not completely *uncommon* for people to seek refuge from the rain at the nearest hotel or motel they can find. Rooms fill up fast."

"I'll call," I offered because Pippa looked about two minutes away from losing her cool.

She turned to face me, skepticism written all over her face. "Can I trust you to actually call?"

I shrugged off the sting of her words. "I said I would, didn't I?"

"You say a lot of things," she shot back.

I sighed and shook my head before I pulled out my phone and looked up a handful of lodging establishments a few miles in either direction. Each one gave me the same answer.

"Sorry we're all booked."

I took a few minutes to steel myself against whatever verbal darts Pippa would throw at me before I went to deliver the bad news. "No vacancies," I told her when I found her scowling at the floor as if she could force it to open up, or catch fire by the sheer force of her will. "None at all. Single or double rooms, not even a suite for twenty miles."

Her delicate shoulders slumped forward in disappointment, or maybe it was resignation that we would be sharing a room for the night. "All right. We'll take the room, then. Thanks."

"It's not so bad, Pip. She said it's a king sized bed, which means it'll be like sleeping in two separate beds."

She snorted and turned to face me as we stood outside the Lover's Suite. "*Like* sleeping in two beds isn't the same as two beds," she growled and shoved the key into the lock. "I'm taking a shower first." She stomped off and I remained silent, knowing that nothing I said would satisfy her at the moment.

The shower turned on and I kicked off my shoes and looked around the place. It was set for romance with the big bed, the deep shades of red that decorated the place, the pillows, the rug in front of the fireplace. Flowers sat in three vases around the room, red and white and pink roses, candles waited to be lit and champagne chilled in a bucket. It was a nice place for a couple in love.

A knock sounded and I found Trixie outside with a smile. "I realized you weren't prepared to stay the night, so I've brought some robes for you and Pippa."

"Oh, thank you, Trixie."

"Of course. And I can toss your clothes in the wash so they're fresh for tomorrow's trip back home."

"Really? That would be great, thanks." I accepted the pile and tossed it on the bed. "One second?"

"Take your time," she offered with a polite smile.

I took my life in my own hands by pushing open the bathroom door to grab Pippa's clothes, folded neatly on the toilet seat, but I figured she would appreciate the clean clothes more than she would resent my sneaking in while she showered. I shucked off my own clothes, tossed them in the cloth bag Trixie had provided in the pile, and handed them off to her with a word of thanks.

And waited for the storm from Pippa.

Luckily, I didn't have to wait long.

"What did you do with my clothes?" Pippa stood in the doorway wrapped in an oversized towel, red hair clinging to her pale skin. "Earth to Ryan! Where are my clothes?"

"Trixie came by and offered to wash them. Left these cozy robes for us." I tossed the fluffy light blue robe in her direction and Pippa fumbled, catching the fabric just as her towel fell around her feet. "Sorry."

"Right," she snarled. "You look incredibly sorry."

I shrugged casually at her words. "I'm sorry you're upset at the nice gesture, but not sorry I got a glimpse of you in your birthday suit."

"Pig," she muttered and tightened the sash around her waist, a move that highlighted her cleavage because the robe was at least two, possibly three sizes too big for her.

"How about I pour us a glass of wine? I'll keep my snout out of your glass, promise." I winked and she growled, actually growled at me.

"Just pour the damn wine," she grunted again and tightened the sash once again for good measure.

"Still bossy as hell, I see." It was one of the things I loved most about her. She was tiny as heck, but with a personality three times as big, not to mention she was always in charge of everyone. All the time.

"Not bossy," she clarified. "Goal oriented."

"I knew you were gonna say that." She hated being called bossy. "Nothin' wrong with a bossy woman. It's damned sexy, let me tell ya." She'd always been the sexiest girl around with her fiery red hair, feminine curves and sassy attitude.

"Plenty of bossy women on tour?"

"That depends," I drawled. "Are you jealous of these fictious bossy women beating down my backstage door?"

"Hardly. Plenty of guys making false promises about forever and *other* things. Don't need a rock star for that."

"Ouch. You wound me, Pip."

"Stop calling me that!" She marched over to the small coffee table and plucked her glass from the table with a grunt. "My name is Pippa, or Ms. Carson is you prefer."

I arched a brow. "Not Mrs. Carson?"

"No," she snarled. "I kept my name because it's *mine*."

I smacked my lips together. "Not very southern of you, Pip."

"Yeah well, I've grown and I don't let things like traditions determine how I live my life anymore. Did that once and it didn't work out too well for me." She took a big, unladylike sip from her glass and sighed loudly. "I suppose that means you have a Mrs. Gregory walking around free in this world?"

"Is that curiosity I hear?"

"Nope," she insisted a little too quickly. Too easily. "Just making conversation since we're stuck here until the rain lets up."

"She might have kept her married name, I don't rightly know. My best guess is she was as eager to get rid of it as she was to get rid of me."

Pippa smacked her lips together in a fake pout. "Were you a bad husband?"

"Absent more than bad." Just thinking about that too short marriage made me mad as hell. "She knew who I was when she married me, and then she punished me because I was on the road, doing the job I did when we met." It was silly to marry Shelby and I could be honest now; I'd done it to forget the woman staring at me from across the Lover's Suite. "I never should have married her."

"Why did you?"

Her blue eyes bore through me as if she could see my truth, as if she knew the only reason I'd married Shelby was because she was a poor substitute for the one woman I never could forget. Not that Pippa would believe me if I said as much to her. "Because I wanted to prove something."

One fiery brow arched in question. "What?"

"That I was over you. That you no longer had a hold on me or my heart."

Pippa's blue eyes shuttered immediately and she buried her face in the glass. "Joke's on you, because I never had a hold on it as it turns out. I was just another place holder. Your first groupie."

Heat infused my body at her words. "That right there is the biggest load of bullshit I've ever heard, and I think you know it." She was unbelievable, so determined to rewrite history. "I loved you more than I have ever loved anyone in my whole life, Pip."

She snorted and finished off her wine, keeping as much distance between us as possible while still grabbing the bottle for a refill. "If that's true, I can see why you and your ex didn't make it. I didn't mean anything to you. First loves are a joke. A fantasy that only seems great under the rose-colored lenses of adolescence."

"You don't believe that."

"I do now." She plopped down on the far end of the sofa. "You cured me of that girlish fantasy, so really, I should thank you. I thought we were so in love, I was mad for you back then." She shook her head, eyes glazed over as if she was back in the past. "I thought we'd have a truckload of babies, live in a big brick house, and I'd get to be your date for every music awards show on the planet, cheering you on while you won award after award."

That had been my dream too, I just hadn't seen how to make it work back then.

"Turns out you had other plans, and they never, not once included me." She shook her head and took a long, fortifying sip that finished half the glass. "I was so hurt, so humiliated. And as time went on, I realized that I never saw us as we really were, not truly."

"That's not true. We were great."

"We were a rite-of-passage. Childhood sweethearts, first sex partners, first heartbreaks, sure. But it was never love and if it was, I'm glad I've steered clear of that trap all these years." She sighed and smiled into the distance, looking proud of herself that she hadn't love anyone in twenty years.

"Not something I'd be bragging about, Pip."

Her nostrils flared again. "I said don't call me that. Nicknames are for friends and we are not friends. We never were," she whispered that last part to herself.

"You were my best friend."

"Ha!" She laughed and laughed, until her face was red and she was out of breath. "That's why you waited until the day before you left for Nashville to tell me you were going and not taking me with you?"

"Pip..."

"I'd hate to see how you treat people you actually give a damn about."

"I loved you," I told her. "I still do."

Her smile faded and her eyes went dark. "You never

loved me, Ryan. I know that, and I don't blame you. We were kids with silly fantasies that were destined to be nothing more than broken promises. We had attraction and chemistry and we thought it was love. Silly, right?"

"I loved you with all my heart and I never stopped."

"No!" She slammed her glass down and the stem cracked. "You didn't. You never did. I was just a fun girl willing to sleep with you, but it wasn't love. Not for you."

I stood and set my glass down. "Don't tell me how I felt, Pip." There was less than a foot between us now. "You can be sore about how things ended up between us, but don't downplay what we had. It was love. The big kind of love that you never forget. That kind that stays with you forever and ever."

"Like a chronic illness," she mumbled into the wine glass."

That was it. My temper flared and I reached out to her, wanting desperately to shake some sense into the stubborn woman. "Does this feel like a chronic illness, Pip?" Her blue eyes widened and I was sure a smart remark was on the tip of her tongue, but my mouth crashed down over hers, consumed her until she was silent. Until she gave in to the heat that always sparked between us. Even when we were mad. Even when she hated me, or wanted to anyway.

Her hands clung to me and then fisted in the fabric of my robe. She moaned when my tongue slid against the seam of her lips, urging them open. Our tongues collided and Pippa melted into me, moaned again. The sound hit me right between the legs and I deepened the kiss, her taste taking me back to a time when she was mine. A time that we were happy and planning for a future that never came to be.

In that moment, there in the Lover's Suite, the past didn't matter. The future didn't matter, the only thing that I cared about was hearing more of those sexy throaty sounds she made when our tongues touched, the way her hands slid beneath my robe and over my shoulders, down my back until the robe hit the ground.

Pippa sucked in a breath and pulled away, her gaze dark as it raked over my body. "Totally unfair," she growled and recaptured my mouth, gliding her tongue back and forth across my lips. Her kisses were more intoxicating than the wine, and I let her take control just to see how far she would take it, but when she nipped my chin and my jaw, that playful sexiness that I remembered so well came back to me in vivid color, and I lifted her in my arms.

She gasped, as if suddenly aware that very little fabric separated us. Specifically, her soft and fluffy robe was the only thing between us, and when I lifted her in my arms, her hot, wet flesh pressed against where I was stiff and aching for her.

"Goodness," she growled and held on to me with one hand while the other roamed my body as if she was trying to remember every inch of me. Every muscle, every dip and plane of my flesh.

One drop was all it took. One little drop of her arousal slid down my belly and that was it, my control snapped. I marched us over to the bed and tossed her down, staring at her because twenty years hadn't changed how gorgeous she was. Long legs, still lean and well-muscled, ample hips and a narrow waist punctuated with tits that were more than a handful. "So fucking gorgeous," I growled and knelt on the bed, eager for a taste of her.

"Ry," she gasped when my shoulders spread her thighs. "You don't...oh!" The words died on her tongue when my tongue slid through her wet folds in a slow up and down motion. Eventually her hips joined in the dance, swirling eagerly as I lapped up her juices and slid my tongue deep inside her. "Oh. Ry."

The way my name fell from her lips left me breathless and excited. She smelled the same as I remembered, she tasted even better, and I couldn't get enough of the combination. Every moan, every cry and every plea that fell from her lips cranked my arousal up to one thousand. My hands gripped her thighs and pushed them apart while I pushed her closer and closer to the edge, eager to hear more sounds of her arousal. Her pleasure.

"Oh. My. God." She squirmed and begged, sang my name like it was her favorite song. Over and over she said my name, begged for me to give her the release she wanted. When I was satisfied with her growls of pleasure, when she was wound so tight she climbed the bed to get away from me, only then did I let her have what she wanted. What she needed and begged for. "Ryan, yes!" Her body went tense for several eternal moments and then she went slack, a satisfied, beautiful smile on her face.

I kissed my way up her body, taking my time over every dip, every curve of her womanly shape. I lingered on her beautiful tits, sucking pretty pink tips until they were hard and aching. "So sweet," I sighed as I reached her mouth. "So damn sexy."

"So, so good," she moaned and when my hips pressed against hers, blue eyes rolled back in her head.

"And it's only about to get better," I promised as I thrust in one long stroke. "Oh, shit." She was tight and hot. "So slick."

"More, Ry. Give me more." She arched into me and the last little thread of my control snapped.

I gave her what she wanted, what we both wanted and needed. It was twenty years of loss, of grief and of longing tied up in our coming together. It was everything that we should have had for the past two decades, only it was better and more intense because we'd been deprived. Every thrust felt like a purging of sins and wrongdoings. Sweat trickled down my forehead with the effort it took to hold back my pleasure, pumping harder and deeper, enjoying the way her nails dug deep into the muscles of my back. "Oh, Pip."

Her body trembled and shook as her tongue swiped up and down the length of my neck. Her teeth nipped at me playfully and I palmed her ass, pumping harder and faster until we both climbed the top of that mountain and we jumped together, tumbling into that dark, erotic abyss together.

Our chests heaved together as we sucked down oxygen and a moment later, our gazes locked. "Wow."

"Right?" I couldn't believe that things were still just as explosive between us as they were back when we were horny teenagers who couldn't get enough of each other.

I knew, then and there, that Pippa and I weren't done. In fact, I was pretty sure that we were just getting started.

CHAPTER 12
PIPPA

"You can't keep ignoring him forever, Pippa. He's your boss and your neighbor. And apparently, now your lover."

"No." I pointed at my smirking best friend, a steely look on my face which she easily ignored. "Not my lover. That was a mistake. An aberration. A one-off." I sat a little taller in my chair, enjoying a cup of coffee with my best friend, something I'd missed often while I was away. "And I can ignore him since he's doing a very good job of ignoring me too." A week had passed since our trip to Gatlinburg and our overnight stay, and since then Ryan had made himself scarce.

Thankfully, blessedly, scarce.

Valona's eyes rounded in surprise. "Really?"

"Yep. It's a relief, really."

"Bull!" Valona shot back, her vehemence taking me by surprise.

"It is. The last thing I want is to do a rehash of that night, or talk about what it means, because it doesn't mean a thing. It was nothing more than proximity and wine."

She quirked a disbelieving brow in my direction. "No residual emotions from your powerful teenage love affair?"

"Nope." My shoulders fell in relief, because this I could answer honestly. "I told Ryan the truth about our relationship, and I think this all happened because he had something to prove."

"And you? Why did you fall into his arms and his bed so easily?"

I shrugged off her question and gave a concise answer. "Because he's still good lookin' as all get out, and it's been too long since I've been pleased by a man."

"And there are no other good looking men in all of Carson Creek?" Valona laughed. "I'm sorry Pippa, but that's just bull and we both know it."

"It was inevitable, I guess. Bound to happen sooner or later because of our history. And when I told him that, in hindsight our relationship was based more on chemistry, sex and teenage hormones than love or affection, he kind of lost it." In the best possible way.

Valona sucked in a breath, her nostrils flared as she

leaned across the kitchen table with a suspicious look. "You don't really believe that, do you?"

"I do." With my chin lifted in defiance, I refused to back down. It had taken years for me to come to this realization, but it was a natural part of the healing process. "High school couples break up all the time, especially before jetting off to higher education or the military or the workforce. Sometimes it's necessity or geography that breaks them up, and it's sad and eventually they get over it. None of that describes my break up with Ryan."

"Pippa, you were over the moon for him."

"I was, and I'm not debating that, but he clearly wasn't over the moon for me. That's the part that offended him."

"Offended the pants off him," she shot back with a short laugh. "And you."

"We weren't wearing pants," I told her. "We were wearing big and fluffy robes. Very nice, if you're looking for a short weekend getaway with a hot young thing."

Her face flushed furiously and she shook her head in denial. "I have no idea what you're talking about."

"Right. Anyway, I think we cleared the air, engaged in some really incredible and ill-advised sex, so there's nothing left to say about it." And whenever I found my mind wandering to other possibilities, alternative endings, I told myself exactly that. "Now I can focus on the restaurant, and he can do whatever he does when he's not around."

"You seriously haven't talked about it? Not even on the ride back from Gatlinburg?"

"Nope. We talked about menu specials, upcoming events and ways he could promote the restaurant using his fame." He'd been surprisingly cooperative about the whole thing which I should've found suspicious at the time, but I was so grateful he didn't want to talk about the previous night that I just went with it.

"You two have to be the most stubborn people on the planet. Is it really so hard to open your big mouths and communicate?" The words came out on an angry growl and I knew her feelings had more to do with what happened with her never-to-be ex than Ryan and me.

"Valona, this isn't the same. We ended decades ago and we were never serious, definitely not married like you were."

"I know," she said on a sigh. "And I'm sorry. You're right. Your situation with Ryan is nothing like mine, except for the fact that you two need to talk, to hash it out for real to see if there's something more than left-over anger and hurt between you."

"The hurt is going to go away Valona, believe me I've tried a lot over the years. I'm not angry."

She snorted and arched a brow. "You're not?"

"Not until he starts saying stupid things like how he

misses me and still loves me. That does piss me off because I hate a liar, and Ryan Gregory is a liar, at least when it comes to me." I finished off my coffee and refilled it right away. "I got over the anger years ago, Val, as soon as I realized that I had placed more importance on our relationship than he did. And then I was just sad."

"And the hurt, where does that come in?"

"How do you feel about trusting a man after what Randy did?" It was the only way to make her understand.

"I'm not thrilled about the idea of dating again, or trusting a man with my heart. Or the girls' hearts."

"Exactly. That's why I'm still hurt because my misperception of our relationship allowed me to go all in with a teenage boy who was never truly serious and that one heartbreak set the stage for future relationship failures. All of them." That was something I wasn't sure I could ever forgive Ryan for doing to me.

"Pip," she said on a sympathetic sigh. "I'm so sorry. I had no idea."

"Because contrary to what it seems like now that I'm back and he's back, I haven't had a reason to bring this up, or think about over the years. I realized it, healed from it, and for the most part, I've moved on. But trust issues don't go away easily."

"Amen to that, sister."

We shared a smile and I shook off the melancholy of thinking about my past relationships and how spectacularly they all failed. "At least I have a job that I love and so far, it's going well."

"Professional success is pretty darn great, isn't it?"

"So good, especially when I thought my days working in fine dining were over." That was the upside of coming back home, far enough away from Chicago that my past wouldn't follow me constantly. "Private room bookings are increasing and we have some events booked months out for wedding rehearsal dinners, bachelor and bachelorette parties, book club dinners, even athletic associations for awards dinners. And Nina is a dream to work with, she's creative and brilliant and fun."

"So you don't regret coming back home?"

"Are you kidding? I love having movie night with you and the girls. The warm weather down here is fantastic compared to frigid winters and icy lake breezes. I'm happy to be back even if I'm not happy how it came about."

"Good. I was worried Ryan's return would send you running for another decade."

"I didn't run because of Ryan, I just kept up with my previous plans because what else was I going to do?"

"Did you ever consider just going to Nashville even though he never asked?"

"No. He didn't ask and that was as clear a hint as any

of his feelings as if he'd just said go the hell away." My heart had been too battered, my ego too bruised, to follow him like a lovesick fool. "What about you, Val? Have you considered dating again?"

She nodded. "I considered it and dismissed it. I know just about every man in town within acceptable dating age range already, which leaves my options severely limited."

"So date someone older than you, or even better, someone younger than you. It doesn't have to be forever, Val."

"Is forever even a thing anymore?"

"Not from my perspective, but fun is still a thing right? We're not dead, so we should be enjoying this stage of our lives. We've earned it, dammit."

"Absolutely." Valona flashed a wide grin and held up her oversized coffee mug and tapped it against mine. "Does that mean you want to go to Wet Whistle tonight and ogle Grady the bartender?"

"Why the hell not?" I felt a little uneasy, being so happy and settled. So content with my life as it was, that I was sure something lurked in the bushes waiting to tear my peace up, limb from limb. I just knew it.

I couldn't exactly pinpoint it, so I continued going about my life for another week, putting one foot in front of the other, smiling at customers and soaking up the praise of my friends and neighbors in town because life was good. Really good.

Despite the fact that I'd made a fatal error in sleeping with my high school boyfriend. Despite the fact that it was so deliciously good that it invaded my thoughts and my dreams. Ryan was back in town and living next door, but still my life was good.

Really darn good.

CHAPTER 13
RYAN

Being with Pippa again, sharing a bed with her, spending hours on end with her, and yeah, even sliding deep inside of her body, it had all unlocked something wonderful, something magical inside of me. Words. No, better than just simply *words*, there were lyrics. Lines and lines of lyrics and music that turned into fully formed songs seemingly overnight.

Songs.

Music.

For the past two weeks I'd spent every day and every single night holed up in my studio, writing and strumming my guitar, playing the piano and digging deep to produce song after song. It felt as if I'd captured a part of myself I'd forgotten existed, the guy who could get so wrapped up in his craft that he forgot about the world around him. Sure, I've been writing songs for the past fifteen years, once I was able to convince the label to let us a play a few that turned into major hits, but not like this.

I hadn't written like this in ages. Not since Pippa was my muse.

"Knock, knock." The familiar voice of my youngest brother, Roman, interrupted my thoughts and my writing, but I was happy to see him after two weeks straight in my studio.

"Sorry we're closed," I told him with a grin before I waved him inside.

"You weren't recording were you? Because it looked like you were daydreaming."

"Not recording," I confirmed and motioned for him to take a seat. "What's up? Bored being free and clear yet?"

"Nah, I had a few meetings with the studio suits, did some photo shoots and spent a few days learning how to surf with Britney in Malibu." He wiggled his eyebrows as if I hadn't already guessed that Britney was one of his temporary romances. "It was a great time. How about you, big brother, learned to have any fun yet?"

"Oh yeah," I deadpanned. "My life is a million instances of fun each day."

"Way to sell it. Pippa is back in town and working for you."

"I'm aware," I told him, my voice thick with annoyance. "Your point?"

Roman held up his hands defensively. "Just making conversation. How's the songwriting coming along?"

"Excellent. I've gotten about a dozen songs recorded over the past two weeks. Some for the band, some for you and some just came to me." It was a beautiful thing, to have the lyrics and the music flow so freely, to come together so easily. "What?"

"Something *is* up." He pointed at me with a knowing smile. "You and Pippa."

"There is no me and Pippa," I growled in response. The stubborn woman had not called or stopped by once in the past two weeks. She had made no effort to reach out to me since our night in Gatlinburg, which stung. A lot. We were next door neighbors, and I had barely caught a few glimpses of her as she left or arrived back at home after work. If not for some work-related emails and calendar reminders, I might have thought she forgot I existed.

"Maybe not, but something is definitely up. I know it."

"Yeah? What makes you such an expert?" I was being a surly son of a bitch and I knew it, but I didn't care. Pippa's stubbornness knocked me off-kilter.

"Only being on the road with you and in the studio with you for the past couple of decades. All of your best songs are about Pippa. Her big blue eyes. Her lush lips and sweet kisses. Laughing with her. Shit man, you've written at least four songs on the sound of her laugh."

"It's a good laugh, but you're wrong."

"Am I?"

"Damn right you are. These songs are mine. My brainchild. My lyrics and my feelings. My music."

"Whoa, hold up big brother, no one is trying to steal your credit or say those beautiful lyrics weren't all you, but they were inspired by her." I opened my mouth to deny it when my stupid baby brother snatched my notebook from the music stand with a teasing laugh.

"Eyes like the hottest part of the fire. The curve of her hips like the smooth curve of the moon." He laughed again and shook his head. "This is all about Pippa, one hundred percent. And this is good stuff, I'm calling dibs on this song."

"It's not a song." Not yet but it would be. Soon.

Roman's smile faded and his eyes turned serious. "Wanna talk about it."

"Nothing to talk about, really."

"Nothing really usually means something," he shot back and kicked his feet up on my piano bench. "Tell me."

"No."

"Come on, Ry, tell me." He laughed when I smacked his feet off the bench. "Just tell me, maybe I can help."

"I don't need any help." Her silence told me that she actually meant those words she said. "She said I never loved her. That our relationship was nothing more than chemistry and teenage hormones."

"Ouch. Is she wrong?"

I glared at my brother, hard. "All the way wrong."

Roman nodded thoughtfully, his gaze never wavered from my own. "Did you tell her that?"

"She's not ready to hear it because she's convinced herself that her narrative is the truth."

"Then it's on you to show her just how wrong she is, Ry."

I shook my head because I knew it wouldn't get me anywhere. Two weeks, and I wasn't any closer to coming up with a plan to spend more time with Pippa, to changing her mind about me. "I'm working on it."

"Working on what?" My sister's voice wafted over the speakers inside the recording booth.

I groaned and glared at my brother. "Did you call Lacey?"

Roman held his hands up defensively, shaking his head despite the big ass grin on his face. "Nope."

"He didn't have to," she growled as she pushed open the recording booth door. "I've been trying to get in touch with you for more than a week. You don't return phone calls anymore?"

"Been busy," I told her and pointed to the guitar resting against my thigh. "Something wrong?"

Her big blue eyes narrowed to slits. "Does something need to be wrong for me to reach out to my kid brothers?" The telltale toe tapping told me I was in trouble. "I wanted to grab lunch, convince you to let me interview you, dig into all the details of your life for my own personal enjoyment. Basic sister stuff."

"You should have reached out to Devon, he handles all that stuff for me."

Lacey sucked in a shocked breath. "I am not calling your assistant to get penciled into your schedule, not when I have your direct number, Ryan Gregory. When I call, you answer. Got it?"

"Yes ma'am." I saluted for good measure, which earned me another glare.

"Back off, Lacey," Roman said as he flung an arm around her. "Ryan's going through some things, writing songs about Pippa again."

"You're not!" Her blue eyes filled with disappointment and fear.

I shrugged.

"Dammit, Ry, please don't go there again. You broke her last time and it was heartbreaking, watching her walk around town with sadness in her eyes, the light gone. She was a shell after you left for Nashville, and then she went and stayed away for twenty years."

"And that's my fault?"

"In part, yeah, it is," she answered easily. "I'm determined to get our friendship back since she's home, and that won't ever happen if you hurt her again."

"Now hold up one damn minute. How am I the bad guy?" I knew why Pippa thought so, but my own sister?

"I never once toyed with her feelings. I loved her." Still did, not that she believed it.

Roman and Lacey looked at each other for a long moment, reminding me of their close bond despite being the oldest and the youngest siblings, and then burst out laughing. It was loud and raucous and far too damned amused for my liking.

"You kind of did, bro," Roman began, a sympathetic glint in his eyes despite his smile. "Did you even ask her to come with us to Nashville?"

"She was going off to college, I couldn't ask her to put her life on hold while we tried to make something of the band." She was too bright, too brilliant to be sidelined for my career.

"Rii-ight," Lacey said with a shake of her head and her patented annoyed sister eyeroll. "Because there are no colleges whatsoever in Nashville. Or Memphis."

Roman pointed at Lacey proudly. "That right there. You messed up big time and you've been paying for it ever since. Time to shit or get off the pot, Ry."

"Elegantly put, as always," I grunted.

Lacey gave Roman a soothing pat on the back. "Crudely spoken, without a doubt, but his point is valid. If you're not planning on forever this time, stay away. Far, far away."

"Being warned off by my own family. That says everything I need to know about what you both think of me."

"Come on, Ry," Lacey insisted. "It's not that. You didn't ask her to go. If you had, you would probably be married now with a house full of kids. Imagine how she felt? So foolish and humiliated."

"It wasn't like that," I roared.

"Maybe not from your perspective, but she stayed in town for weeks after you left and the whole town knew you'd just left her behind, discarded her like she didn't matter." Lacey shook her head. "It's not about being the good guy or bad, it's about action. And you need her to help your restaurant succeed, remember that."

I sighed because, as usual, Lacey was right. Mostly. I wasn't playing with Pippa, never had been and never would. But I had to tread carefully given this new information. "What's this about an interview?"

Lacey, the head writer and editor at the local paper, Carson Creek Daily Journal, perked right up. "You have time?"

"For my nosy big sister? Always."

"You're the best, Ry."

I quirked a brow at her words. "Just not good enough for Pippa?"

She growled and rolled her eyes. "I think you two are perfect for each other actually. But I think you'll have an uphill battle on your hands getting her to agree to give you a second chance."

"I'm rich. I'm handsome and I'm charming."

"All good things, except for you're also the guy who

broke her heart. That's not easy to come back from, trust me."

"So tread carefully?"

"Very carefully," she agreed. "If she leaves again I won't be able to save you from Valona and Chase."

"He's the mayor," Roman added unnecessarily. "He could probably have you tossed in jail or buried in the Smokies."

"Get out now, or I'll write a bunch of cheesy pop songs for you."

"You wouldn't!"

"Do you want to find out, or do you want your first solo endeavor to top the charts?"

Roman held his hands up with a cheeky smile as he walked backwards out of the recording booth. "Consider me as good as gone. We'll talk soon, Ry. We still on for onion rings and pool at Wet Whistle tonight, Lacey?"

Lacey gave an eager nod. "And potato skins. Possibly dancing."

Roman and I both frowned. "Who are you, and what have you done with our sister?"

"Stevie is out of town with her friends tonight, which means I'm going to kick off my shoes and have a good time, especially with a hot rocker as my wingman." She winked at Roman, who wisely, stayed silent and then bolted for the door. "I'm a forty year old single mother, Ryan. But I'm not dead."

"You're forty-five, and I know you're not dead. You're beautiful and lively, I just wasn't sure if *you* realized it."

Her expression softened and she wrapped me in a tight hug. "I'm so glad to have you back," she groaned and squeezed just a little tighter. "Now tell me, are you really home to write an album or get Pippa back?"

"Didn't realize it was an either or type of situation."

Her blue eyes widened in surprise. "I knew you were more than just a pretty face and soulful lyrics."

"Gee thanks, sis."

Lacey's laugh turned to a sigh. "I want you to know that I'm rooting for you, Ryan. Both of you."

That meant more to me than I could say, so I gave her a tight squeeze and a noogie. "Thanks, Squirt."

Like I knew she would, Lacey shoved me away and punched my shoulder. "Small but not too small to kick your butt. Remember that."

"You could try," I teased. "But do you really want to embarrass yourself like that again?"

"You caught me off guard last time," she insisted with a laugh. "Never again."

I sighed with contentedness because it was damn good to be home. "You want to fight or you want to do your interview?"

"Are they mutually exclusive?"

"Brat," she muttered before pulling out her notebook, turning on her recorder app and peppering me with questions for the next ninety minutes.

CHAPTER 14
PIPPA

"This place is pretty lively for a Thursday night." I looked around Wet Whistle with fresh, new eyes. "The last time I was here I think that jukebox played actual cassette tapes." That wasn't the only change. All the dark cherry wood had been replaced with a blond pine, lighting it up along with the royal blue booth and chair seats, and the bar stools. Instead of old pioneer décor, the place looked like a hipster saloon.

Valona snorted. "Now the music is all digital, and there are at least ten craft brews on tap, if you can believe it."

"A lot has changed in twenty years."

"It happened right in front of me and I'm still amazed." Val grinned as if she was seeing the place for the first time. "My favorite is that the dart boards are all digital now, no more finger counting during five-oh-one."

"You want to play?"

"No, but I am thinking about joining the dart league that meets up here once a week. It'll give me a hobby, and maybe I'll get a practice board for the garage."

"Perfect!" I clapped excitedly. "We can get drunk in the comfort of your home and play darts horribly."

"Speak for yourself, I plan to play perfectly," she shot back with a playful smile. "Don't look now, but two of the four Gregory siblings have just entered the establishment."

My brows dipped in confusion. "Are they not allowed out?"

"Of course they are, why wouldn't they be?" She whispered.

I shrugged and sipped my bourbon. "I don't know, Val. Why are you talking like a spy from the sixties?"

She laughed, and I was pretty sure the bourbon had gone straight to her head. "They're coming this way."

I opened my mouth to ask her which of the two siblings were here just as Lacey appeared, Roman at her side. "Lacey. Roman. Good to see you both."

Surprise flashed in Lacey's blue eyes and she gave me a curt nod. "Glad to have you back in town, Pippa."

"Yeah, Pip. Glad to hear you finally got enough of cold winters and wet summers." Roman bent down and smacked a loud kiss to my cheek, wrapping me in his arms. "Looking like a million bucks as always, Pip."

Strange enough, it didn't bother me when Roman called me Pip. In fact, it brought back so many fun and exciting childhood memories of us swimming at the pond on the edge of town, drinking beers late into the night at Cranston Field, cruising for the sake of cruising. "Right back at you, rock star. You're all grown up."

His cheeks turned the faintest shade of pink. "That happens over twenty years, Pip."

"Right."

Roman turned his attention to Val, giving her a long perusal, his blue eyes filled with heat. "Hey Valona. Looking beautiful. You gonna let me take you out while I'm in town?"

She blinked in confusion that cleared quickly. "Roman," she sighed. "I'm old enough to be-,"

He cut her off. "Old enough to be my sister or my date, I know how old you are. What I don't know, is what night I'm picking you up."

"Damn," I whispered, watching the man I'd known as a little boy, put some smooth moves on my best friend."

"Be serious," she shot back, half annoyed and half angry for some reason.

"I am serious, Valona. If you're not interested just say so. I'm a big boy. I can take it."

"You certainly aren't a boy anymore," I mumbled

with a laugh. Valona shot me a look that told me to shut my mouth. "What? He's hot and fun, and only looking for a good time. Exactly the kind of fun you need."

"Yeah," Roman agreed. "All of that." He winked at me and I rolled my eyes. "So?"

"You are hot. Really hot."

"I think I'm gonna be sick," Lacey said, adding a gag for good measure.

"But I can't," she said with true regret. "Bridget has three posters of you on her wall and that would be weird and unsettling, and it would probably make her hate me."

Roman nodded with a hint of disappointment that I was sure he would shrug off quickly. "Well your daughter has excellent taste. Too bad though, because you look like quite the snack, Val." He shrugged once again and sauntered off.

"Well that was appropriately awkward." Lacey took a sip of her margarita and I realized in that moment how much I'd missed our friendship.

"That's Roman for ya," I added with a grin to ease some of the tension. "Congrats Lacey, I hear you run the paper now."

"Thanks. If I can increase readership and ad revenue, I'll be happy Dad has finally retired."

A loud whistle sounded from the back of the bar and then Roman spoke. "Get your butt over here Lacey, or I'm gonna have a belly full of your potato skins."

She rolled her eyes. "Baby brother calls. It was good to see you both, maybe we could have lunch or dinner, or just a bottle of something expensive together?"

"That sounds wonderful. Girl talk and booze, two things I've sorely missed."

That got her shoulders to relax before she hurried off with a loud warning to stay away from her potato skins for her brother.

"That was nice of you, to break the tension with Lacey. She thought you hated her after you and Ryan broke up."

"I always liked Lacey, and it wasn't her fault. It was just hard to talk to her, to hear about Ryan, so I just let the friendship fall off, which I regret." And now that I was back in town, I could reclaim that friendship too.

Val's green eyes went wide just as the air in the place crackled and sizzled. "A third Gregory sibling just walked in."

"Ryan," I guessed easily.

"Got it in one."

I groaned and let my head fall forward before I looked up at the cracked ceiling. "Why did he have to show up here on my first night out in ages?"

"I don't think that cracked paint is going to answer, at least not before he makes it to the table." She pointed at the ceiling and grinned. "The universe is sending you all kinds of signals that you seem determined to ignore because you are as stubborn as they come."

I heard her words, but all I heard was her say that Ryan was headed towards our table. "No, he's not." I panic-whispered, but Valona only nodded with a far too amused smile.

"Yes," she whispered and then flipped her smile up a few watts. "Ryan, hi. Good to see you."

"You too, Val. Sorry about Randy."

"Don't be," she waved off his condolences. "How are you?"

"Mostly good, been in my studio for the last few weeks writing and that feels good. You?"

"Can't complain, just working to get my photography business off the ground."

"Yeah? You should talk to Roman, he might need a local photographer soon." He turned to me, expression serious. "Can we talk?"

I stiffened at his abrupt change in topic. "Nothing to talk about that can't wait until I'm back on the clock."

"Pippa, please."

"You know what?" Val slid from the booth and straightened her tall frame. "I need to check in on the girls, I'll be back in a few minutes." As soon as the traitor scampered off, Ryan took her seat and leaned half way across the table.

"You've been ignoring me."

"No, I have been working to make your restaurant a success, because it's my job. If anyone has been ignoring anyone, it's you who ghosted on your own investment."

"Maybe," he conceded. "Maybe I did take some space because I knew you wouldn't be receptive to talking about that night in Gatlinburg, but I've had time to think about it."

"Two weeks," I added because my inner smartass wouldn't have it any other way.

"Okay, I had two weeks to think about it and I'm done letting you off the hook, Pip. I'm ready to talk about it and what comes next."

What comes next. I let out a loud, completely unladylike bark of laughter. "*You're* ready to talk about it, so we talk about it? Is that how things work in your world now?" I shook my head unwilling to learn that he was a spoiled rich prick who dictated terms to everyone around him. "Get over yourself, Ryan. There is nothing to talk about. Gatlinburg was nothing more than a lapse in judgment, a screw for old time's sake."

"It's you I haven't gotten over, Pip. Not ever."

Nice words, if I was still the silly little girl so desperate to believe them. "There's nothing to get over anymore, Ryan. You were happy to leave me behind when it mattered, so how about you channel that part of yourself and walk away. Now."

"I made a mistake back then, Pip. I was a stupid kid. What's your excuse for being so damn stubborn and scared now?"

My nostrils flared at his words and anger pulsed in my veins, but I reached for every ounce of cool I could muster and looked him directly in his handsome face. "I'm not stubborn. I'm just not so blindly in love with you that I'm willing to believe every syllable that falls from your lips." My voice grew louder and people started to stare, so I blew out a breath and sat back, flashing my *nothing to see here, folks* smile. "Have a good night, Ryan. Roman and Lacey are at the dart boards."

He flashed a wickedly sexy smile at me. "At least I got you to call me Ryan."

"I'm off the clock, don't read anymore into it than that. Now, please, go away."

"I will. For now, Pip, but this isn't over. Not by a long shot."

"To you maybe, but to me it's been over since that day you walked away from me on the town green." I flashed my most professional restaurant worker smile and waited for him to do what he did best. Walk away.

"I'll let you have what you think you want, for now. But I'll be seeing you soon, Pip. Real soon." He pushed out of the booth that was too small for his big body and finally gave me what I asked for.

Too bad watching him walk away now, hurt as much as it did twenty years ago. Except this time, his words felt more like a threat or a warning, than goodbye.

CHAPTER 15
RYAN

Was there anything better than an ice-cold beer on a hot day after spending all morning in the studio laying down new tracks? Not as far as I was concerned.

The day was still young enough to enjoy, but I'd already put in a good five hours of writing, tweaking and recording. I still had months before the studio expected anything from The Gregory Brothers, so I enjoyed taking my time, playing with new sounds and mixing genres. Some of the songs weren't right for the band, I knew that as I laid them down, but figured I'd give Roman dibs on them before selling them off.

Writing again was good. More than that, it felt good. I hadn't written much during the tour because I was too exhausted, my mind too cluttered and unfocused. I didn't want to think that Pippa had anything to do with it, but I could admit to myself that sparring with her was better than regular conversation with just about anybody else.

"I must be crazy," I told myself as I twisted the cap off a bottle of stout. The woman clearly hated me, at least on the surface. She couldn't hate me too much if she'd slept with me, but her walls were a mile high where I was concerned, and getting anything from her other than physical satisfaction seemed to be close to impossible.

Still I wanted her as much as I ever had.

A knock sounded on the door and I smiled at the sound of quick, angry taps on the front door because I knew my mind had conjured up the woman who occupied my thoughts day and night. I took my time, taking long relaxed strides towards the front of the house. After a sip of beer and a relaxed sigh, I pulled the door open with a smile.

"Pippa, finally come to your senses?" I knew I shouldn't tease her, but it was just too much fun.

Pippa's nostrils flared and her jaws clenched tight, but she said nothing at first, just smacked a stack of envelopes against my chest. "Your mail came to my house." She turned on her heels as if she couldn't get away fast enough, which stung just a little.

"Too chicken shit to stay?"

She froze in the middle of the porch steps but kept her back to me even as she folded her arms across her chest in a defensive gesture. "And what do I have to be afraid of?"

"Your attraction to me. Obviously." The smile in my tone made her turn to face me, a skeptical look on her beautiful face.

Pippa rolled her eyes. "I am not a horny teenage girl anymore Ryan, and you are not exactly irresistible."

I put a hand to my chest and staggered back. "You wound me, Pip."

"Then I suggest you go find some groupie to massage your ego. I'm sure there are no shortage of those." Her words were sharp enough, but I couldn't help but poke her a little more.

"Jealous?"

"Hardly. I have no plans to massage your ego, or any other part of you for that matter."

"That's good because I'd rather have a tongue lashing from you than an ego massage from anyone else. "Beer?"

"No thanks. I have things to do." She turned away and marched down the steps as I clucked like a chicken behind her. "That won't work on me, maybe try a younger woman."

"I already got my eye on one, she's just being difficult."

A growl escaped from her, and the sound was dark, low and sexy as hell. I kept my gaze fixed on her mighty fine backside as she stomped across my yard and then hers, climbing the steps two at a time before she slammed her front door shut with more energy than the task required.

I smiled and went back inside, but the icy beer wasn't as appealing anymore. The silence wasn't as welcoming now that Pippa had spiked my heartrate with just her presence. Her sharp tongue.

I made it a full hour before I could no longer resist the pull of Pippa. I took a cold shower that turned hot, and I found myself scouring the bar for the bottle I knew would get me in the door. That's how I found myself armed with Maker's Mark, two rocks glasses, and standing on her doorstep.

She pulled the door open and rolled her big blue eyes towards the sky with a heavy sigh. "Ryan. What's up?"

I held up the bottle and glasses. "The stars will start to pop soon and I figured we could drink until we're no longer enemies while we stargaze." I swung the bottle temptingly until she laughed reluctantly.

"And if I say no?"

I shrug. "I'll just lay out in my own backyard and talk to you over the fence. Either way we're stargazing together, Pip."

"Stop calling me that."

I stepped inside and forced her to step back, and I even pretended not to notice the hitch in her breath. "Why do you hate it so much?"

"Because I'm not that naïve little girl anymore, Ryan.

Pip doesn't exist anymore, and you calling me that just reminds me of how silly I used to be, so stop calling me that, damn you."

"You'll always be Pip to me. That girl with the wild red hair, always willing to strip down and take a dip in the lake, let her hair blow wild with the convertible top down."

"*Stolen* convertible," she reminded me with a hint of a smile.

"Borrowed," I clarified as my own smile grew bigger.

"Yeah well, that girl put her whole heart into everything she did and ended up hurt. A lot. This woman protects herself first."

"You know what I think?"

Pippa turned on her heels and rushed through the living room and the kitchen, she didn't stop until we were in the backyard. "I don't care what you think Ryan, but I doubt that will stop you."

I laughed and set down the glasses to fill them each halfway. "I think you've been protecting yourself for so long that you don't even know what you're protecting yourself from anymore."

"I know exactly from what, and whom, I'm protecting myself." She shook her head and picked up one glass, raising it in a reluctant cheers before she tossed it back in two gulps. "I put everything into our relationship and planning for our future, and you weren't even thinking about having me in your future. I put years into that restaurant in Chicago, doing everything I could to make sure customers had a wonderful experience, and some angry son of a bitch cost me that job. Time and time again, I give and give, and get nothing in return. No, I get less than nothing, so I protect myself because apparently I'm the only person who won't hurt me!" She slammed the glass down and motioned for me to fill it again.

"Never pegged you for a victim."

"Yeah well, me neither, but that's life sometimes. I've learned my lesson the hard way so you can damn well bet it's a lesson I won't soon forget."

I nodded, because I heard what she didn't say explicitly. She hadn't forgotten what I did, and she didn't plan on revisiting memory lane with me. "I'm sorry, Pip. So damn sorry."

She shrugged like it didn't matter, but I knew that it did. "It's water under the bridge, Ryan. I forgave you years ago."

I nearly spat my drink out at her words. "I'd hate to see how you treat people you don't forgive."

"I forgave you because I didn't want to hang on to that anger, not because I was no longer hurt, but I couldn't hang on to that hurt and move on with my life. So I forgave you because I had to."

"Doesn't seem like you've forgiven me."

"Because I don't want to just pick up where we left off twenty years ago? Typical man."

"Because I can still feel the hate and anger you have towards me, Pip."

"It's not you," she admitted, shoulders hanging low as she swirled the alcohol in her glass. "Seeing you reminds me of how stupid and naïve I was back then, and I hate it. I'm sorry for taking that out on you."

Her words surprised me even more than a backhand across the face would have. "You weren't stupid, Pip. Or naïve."

"I was," she insisted and shook her head as if that alone could block my words.

"No, you were wonderful. So beautiful and free and open. No one ever loved me the way you did, Pip. You made me realize that it was okay to show that love to another person, hell you made me long for that kind of love when we were apart. I've never loved anyone else like that. It was a gift."

"And a curse," she grumbled with a sad, almost wistful sigh like maybe she missed it too.

"Yeah, a curse too, because losing you and that feeling, makes me terrified as hell that I'll never get it again." I stepped in close to her, that floral scent pulled me close enough that I could smell the whisky on her breath. "That maybe you were my one shot at having that kind of love and I managed to screw it up."

"Ryan," she sighed and tried to take a step back, but I pulled her closer, one arm banded around her lower back. "Please."

"I mean it, Pip." I don't know who moved forward first, me or Pippa, but a moment later our lips were fused together, the kiss started off inferno-hot, twenty foot flames of desire swirled around us, making my skin damp with sweat and desire. Pippa didn't back away from the kiss either, she wrapped her arms tight around me and pressed her delicious curves against my body like she too couldn't get enough.

She moaned into my mouth and the sound of her pleasure cracked my willpower in half. All I wanted in the world in that moment was to hear her make that sound over and over again. She pulled back with a sigh, blue eyes glazed over with desire, eyelids heavy with need. "We shouldn't."

"Probably," I breathlessly agreed. "But we will."

She nodded. "Yeah." And put her mouth to mine again, almost as if she was throwing caution to the wind and choosing to be with me, at least in this moment.

Coming together this time should have been calmer, more sedate since we'd already done this once before recently. But it wasn't calm or sedate, or any other word that didn't mean wicked and wildly out of control.

Pippa tore at my clothes the same way I tore at hers, fabric ripping in our hurry to get naked and come together before the fire burned us completely. When she was naked, I took a step back, still unable to believe that twenty years had passed and she still looked so perfect.

"Pippa, sweetheart, you are a painting. No, even

better, a song." I could hear the strains of that song as I pressed kisses on every inch of her skin, a low drumbeat as her body vibrated each time my lips landed on her overheated skin. Quiet, gravelly moans as I found my way to her core made up the chorus of the song.

Every cry, every moan, every shudder, came together in perfect harmony. "Ry," she growled when I pushed into her body, rocking slowly to build her up. Gasping breaths, heaving chests, skin smacking together combined with the sounds of crickets and frogs in the distance.

It was absolutely perfect.

Our bodies fit together perfectly, moved in sync to give and to receive as much pleasure as we could. Pip arched into me and dug her heels deep, urging me to give her more. "Pip," I growled when another, taller flame of fire licked at my skin and my spine tensed along with my sac.

Her lips curled into a smile. "Yeah?"

"Yeah," I grunted.

She licked her lips and pulled me down so our foreheads touched. "Let go, Ryan. Let's see if you still remember how."

The challenge in her words fired me up and I took her mouth, kissing her deeply. My tongue flicked in tune with every thrust of my hips, growing faster and more frantic with every thrust. I went deeper and she got wetter, driving me out of my mind. Her legs tightened around my waist and she nibbled my bottom lip with a moan. "Pip," I grunted again and again as my mind grew full of this woman, her sounds and the way her skin flushed when she was turned on.

When she was close.

My fingertips dug into her hips and she met me, stroke for stroke, limbs tangled as we both fell over that mountaintop together, gasps mingling on the air and added to the beauty all around us. "My goodness," she said on a laugh mixed with an exhale.

"Your goodness, indeed."

She fell back against the grass and laughed. A genuine laugh flushed her skin even further.

And I could only think of one thing.

There she is, the girl I fell in love with and never fell out.

CHAPTER 16
PIPPA

I did it again. Somehow my clothes fell off and I ended up doing the naked dance with my high school boyfriend. Again.

It was wonderful. No, wonderful was too tame a word for the way Ryan made my body feel. It was hot and magnificent, it was really intense like two lovers reunited after decades apart.

Which is the truth, my mind added sarcastically.

I sighed with satisfaction, ignoring the cooling ground underneath my body. He was an old lover, but sex with Ryan wasn't like it had been back then when we couldn't get enough of each other. This wasn't just both of us being insatiable, horny teenagers, happy to just be naked with someone else. This was magnetic, it was explosive. It was almost as if once we touched—lips or fingertips, it didn't matter—there was no stopping the inevitable progression of what came next.

White-hot sex, that's what came next.

Always.

"That's a whole lot of thinkin' when I've just boinked your brains out." Ryan's deep, amused voice came from right beside me, his fingertips brushing against my sensitive skin.

"Boinked?"

"Banged seemed to crude, and screwed seemed too juvenile."

He was right, on both accounts. "Then I guess boink shall stand."

"So, you gonna tell me what's on your mind?"

You. "Nope."

"Regrets?"

"No," I answered on a sigh. My life would be a hell of a lot easier if I did. "I don't regret it, even if I probably should."

"Because you still hate me, Pip?"

I cringed at his continued use of the name I hated so much. "We already talked about this. I don't hate you."

"Then why regret an evening of fantastic sex?" He made it sound so simple, and though I was nobody's prude, it just didn't *feel* that simple.

"Why? The same reason I hate hearing you call me Pip." I hated the fact that I still wanted Ryan, that as much as looking at him hurt, being with him felt too good to deny. "It's not about you, it's about the me I am when I'm with you."

"I don't know, sweetheart, that still sounds like it's about me."

I turned my gaze up to him with a smile. "That's just your rockstar ego."

He laughed, the sound deep and rich as he pulled me so that my back was flush up against the front of his naked body. "Nobody keeps me grounded like you, Pip."

In that moment, I closed my eyes and inhaled his masculine, slightly musky from sex, scent. I let myself live in that one moment, in his arms, contented and satisfied after sex. And for just a few moments, I let myself be Pip, the spunky girl who had no idea how cruel the world, and men, could be. "That's because I know you don't walk on water."

He gave me a quick squeeze. "That can be our little secret."

"No one would believe me anyway."

His lips brushed against my neck, his teeth nibbled gently at my earlobe. "God, Pip, I just can't get enough of you."

I smiled at his words, but I knew they weren't true. "You will."

He froze for just a moment but it was noticeable. "You'll never forgive me for going after my dreams, will you Pip?"

I inched out of Ryan's grasp and focused on his face

to see if he was kidding, if he was just trying to get a rise out of me again, but his expression was dead-on serious. Almost bewildered.

"You still don't get it, do you?"

He sat up, his golden chest nearly glistening in the moonlight. "I guess you'll have to enlighten me, darlin'."

My gaze narrowed and I pointed an angry finger at him. "Don't give me that *darlin'* crap Ryan, and don't bat your damn eyelashes at me.

His eyes widened innocently and he put a hand to his chest. "Who me?"

I nod defiantly. "Yeah, you. You've already gotten what you want," I sighed, "so there really is no point in rehashing the past."

"What *I* wanted? I seem to remember, very vividly, you enjoyed yourself too. Unless, was that me pushing my own head down and begging for more?"

"What can I say? You have a talented mouth, but we're not talking about me. You got exactly what you came here for, that's what I'm talking about."

"That's not why I came here Pippa, I just wanted to see you. To hear your laugh."

"Okay, fine. You got that too, now it's time for you to go." This man was a professional songwriter, he had a knack for words and could put them together in a way that might make me forget our past.

He laughed and pushed off the ground quickly.

"Dammit, getting off that hard ground ain't as easy as it used to be." He looked down at me determinedly. "I'm not going anywhere until we talk Pip. For real. So let's stop with the anger and just enlighten me, will ya?"

He wanted to talk about this? Then I would make sure he heard the truth, cold and unvarnished. "I'm not mad that you went to chase your dreams, Ryan. I was always your biggest cheerleader. I wanted you to go out and become the star you are today. I was upset that you never once even asked me if I wanted to come with you, almost as if you hadn't even *considered* it." The fact that I was less than an afterthought to him was what hurt most. "Did it even occur to you to ask?" Did I really want the answer to that now, after all these years? *Hell no.* I put my hands up to stop any words about to fall from his lips. "Okay. You've been enlightened and now it's really time for you to go." I picked up my tank top and slipped it over my head before I went in search of my cut-off shorts.

"Pippa," he began, but no words followed and that was all the answer I needed.

"It's all right, Ryan. I don't need an explanation. Not anymore."

"Then what do you need?"

I sighed. "I need you to stop trying to rewrite history, to stop pretending that we were some great love story when the truth is that you dropped the dead weight as soon as you got the chance. That's what makes me angry, Ryan. I can't tell if you're being cruel or just oblivious, but I don't like it at all."

The weight of his stare pressed down on my shoulders until guilt started to creep in, but I held strong. I watched him carefully as he took his time getting dressed, admiring the way his body still moved with the grace of a man half his age. Ryan stopped in front of me and leaned in to kiss me, laughing gently when I gave him my cheek.

"All right, Pip. I'm going. For now."

I nodded because there was nothing else to say.

He stopped at the gate in the fence and turned to me, a sad, slightly disappointed look on his face. "For what it's worth, Pip, I did think of asking you. Thought long and hard about it for a few weeks, but I didn't want you to give up your dreams for me. We both deserved to go after our dreams, sweetheart."

I wanted to believe him, but I couldn't. I just did not believe him. "Bull. There are still colleges in Nashville to this day. Memphis too. I wouldn't have had to give up my dreams, I could have chased them right alongside you. The truth that it took me a long time to see, is that you couldn't wait to be rid of me so you could be free to bang your way through Nashville, which I'm sure you did. So, congratulations." Just thinking of how easily, how quickly he walked away when I'd been planning for our future, stung. My eyes burned with unshed tears and I rushed inside and slammed the door.

He didn't get it and he never would. I had to face those facts all over again and that had me questioning my decision to return to Carson Creek.

CHAPTER 17
RYAN

Pippa was giving me the cold shoulder, but it was the real cold shoulder, not that passive aggressive thing women did where they *want* you to know that they were ignoring you on purpose. No, she was polite and civil whenever we spoke, she answered my questions when absolutely necessary, but only about the restaurant. It was annoying, and worse, my anger started to get the best of me.

"Is there anything else you need, Mr. Gregory?"

I sucked in a breath at her words and my nostrils flared. My pulse sped up as fury roared through my veins. "I've been buried deep inside you and you're still addressing me like we're strangers?"

Pippa, for her part, gave a defiant nod, her expression bewildered like I was the one out of line. "Sex is an intimate act, but that doesn't make us *not* strangers Ryan."

"Crazy damn woman," I grumbled and walked out of the manager's office inside Dark Horse. I felt the curious stares of employees on me. But I ignored them all and stepped out into the Tennessee sunshine to jump in to my truck. I needed to talk to someone, and I had just the person in mind.

I found a parking spot just off Main Street and walked the block and a half to the Carson Creek Daily Journal offices where my sister spent her days. I stopped at the reception desk to make sure Lacey was in, but her loud, amused laughter caught my attention before the words left my mouth.

I frowned at her all too amused expression. "And just what the hell is so funny?"

"You," she pointed and gasped with laughter. "Another fight with Pippa?"

"Is it that obvious?"

Lacey shrugged. "Only because I've seen that expression many, many times. Want to talk about it?"

I nodded and she motioned for me to follow her into her office that used to be our dad's for decades before he finally retired. Sort of retired, anyway. I dropped down in the comfortable leather chair with a sigh. "I just can't win with that woman."

"Maybe stop trying to *win* and start being honest about what you really want."

"I can't," I growled, still angry that Pippa had reverted back to her perfect imitation of a robot. "I thought I'd see her again and it would be weird for a minute, and then we'd become some sort of friends and go on about our lives. But that didn't happen, dammit. She still does it for me Lacey." Which I could live with if she didn't hate my guts.

Lacey nodded, her lips curled into a small, sympathetic smile. "What you need to do, dear brother, is make up for the past and do it properly. Once you do that, show her that you want her outside of the bedroom too."

I frowned across the big desk that had been there for as long as I could remember. "Who said anything about the bedroom?"

"Oh come on, Ry. I remember you two the first time around, as soon as you started getting naked together you couldn't get enough of each other. You skipped over the apology part and went straight to the sex, and she probably thinks that's all you wanted."

I nodded at her accurate assessment of Pippa's perspective. "How in the hell am I supposed to make up for the past? I can't apologize because that would mean saying I did something wrong, and I didn't."

Lacey rolled her eyes and let out a low, almost frustrated groan. "Pippa was always your biggest fan, Ry. I highly doubt she's upset that you left, more like that you left without her."

"People keep saying that," I roared angrily and smacked the desktop with my palm. "I thought I was doing the right thing back then."

She held up her index finger. "Bob and Marcy Johnson both left for Belmont University and they've been married for a decade. Tim Cranston and Jenny Welliver went to Vanderbilt together and broke up sophomore year." She held up a third finger with a smug expression. "Jeremiah Wright transferred from U of Memphis to Austin Peay to be with Kelly and they married before graduation, have two kids and are still going strong." She flashed another smug smile. "Should I keep going?"

"Are there more?"

Lacey shrugged and sat up, her gaze practically bored into my own. "This is a small town, so yeah, there are plenty. Many of them are married with kids, a few are divorced, and the rest figured out pretty quickly that they were only meant to be high school sweethearts. Your actions denied you and Pippa the chance to figure out which group you'd fall into."

"It might be too late to figure that out."

"Well, the sex and the arguments indicate that you're something more than *former* high school sweethearts, even now."

"So you're saying it's not too late?" That gave me hope that there was something I could do to make Pippa less angry and more willing to listen.

"If you think it's too late, leave her be and hook up with one of the local groupies hoping to get a piece of you."

I winced at her words. "No, thanks."

"Look Ryan, I know women have been easy for you over the years, but even when Pippa was head over heels in love with you, she wasn't easy. Why should she be now?"

That was a good question, one I had no answer for. "I don't know, I just thought it would be easier than it's been."

"In the words of our old man, nothing worth having comes easy."

Pippa was definitely worth it, which meant I needed to put in more work. "So I need to apologize?"

"Only if you mean it."

I nodded. "Thanks, Lacey."

"What are older, wiser sisters for?"

I laughed and looked around the mostly empty office. "How are things going around here?"

"All right," she sighed. "Dad still thinks he's in charge, and so he's delaying my efforts to start an online version to increase subscriptions and bringing in guest writers."

"Just do it. If I've learned one thing over the years, it's better to ask forgiveness than permission. One always comes eventually, but the other may never come."

Lacey let out a long breath with a genuine smile. "Thanks, Ryan."

"I can be wise too."

She laughed. "I'll believe it when I see it."

Yeah, me too.

CHAPTER 18
PIPPA

"Hey Pippa, come and try this white truffle risotto with butternut squash. It's got a twist, and I think it'll be a good special since it's supposed to cool down today." Nina smiled in my direction, a large silver spoon in her hand.

I hadn't eaten all day and Nina's food was spectacular, so I made my way over to the stove and stopped halfway when my stomach flipped. The smell was divine of course, but the closer I got the more queasy I felt. I pushed through it, reminding myself not to skip breakfast again.

"All right let's try this masterpiece."

Nina's face brightened. "I added roasted garlic and smoked some cayenne peppers. Let me know what you think?" Her gaze remained fixed on me as I accepted the oversized bite. The flavors popped individually to create an excellent bite.

Then my stomach turned over. And I took off, desperate to reach the bathroom before the risotto made a return appearance. I made it with just a few seconds to spare, retching and heaving long after the risotto came back up. "Whoa."

"Was it the risotto?" Nina's concerned voice startled me, but it shouldn't have since she was a sweetheart.

"No. The risotto was wonderful and I think it's going to be a hit tonight. I think I'm coming down with something." I'd ignored the signs over the past couple days, the exhaustion and sore muscles. "Maybe I'm working too much."

"How about I whip you up a hearty stew?"

My stomach rumbled and threatened another lurch. "How about a nice flavorful broth?"

Nina scoffed. "I'll get a nice consommé going because I am not a neanderthal." She flashed a playful smile and left the employee bathroom, giving me the privacy I needed to get myself back together.

Since the kitchen was off limits for a while, I went back to my office and got an early start on payroll. With every scroll down the screen, my eyes started to swim, which started a headache behind my eyes. By the time I finished the last employee, I had a full-blown migraine that for some reason, worsened the nausea I thought was gone with the risotto. "I can't do this," I said to myself out loud because I needed to believe it. I couldn't finish my shift today which meant I needed help.

Ryan knew nothing about running a restaurant and he was the last person I wanted to see anyway, so I called in a much more capable option. "Devon, do you think you can fill in for me tonight?"

An hour later, Devon strolled into the restaurant wearing a deep blue three piece suit, complete with pocket square and socks that matched his tie. "Oh Pippa, you look terrible. Sorry."

"Don't be, I feel even worse than I look." It wasn't uncommon to pick up every seasonal sickness that came into the restaurant, especially when I worked too many hours and didn't get enough fuel. "Payroll is done. The specials need to be printed up and posted online. I left a list beside the keyboard."

"Consider it all taken care of. Get some rest and let me know how you feel in the morning."

I smiled, grateful for his kindness and willingness to fill in on such short notice. "Thank you, Devon. I owe you one."

I made my way home in a fog of sickness, not quite sure how I made it to the right place without getting into an accident. I kicked the door closed and shed my shoes and clothes on my way to the sofa, where I stayed for the next two hours. Or more.

Sometime later a knock sounded on the door and

Valona strolled in. "Hey honey, word around town is that you're not feeling well."

"Is that the kind of gossip that's going around these days? Pathetic," I joked to ease my best friend's worry.

"No, but Devon called to let me know you looked like death warmed over. His words, not mine."

I had to laugh at that. "Compared to Devon, I always look terrible."

"Right? I always feel more like a hobo than a hippie when he's around." She took one look at me and her brows furrowed with worry. "Oh Pippa, you don't look good at all."

"Well, there goes my dreams of breaking into the fashion industry as a middle aged supermodel."

Val went into mommy mode, pressing the back of her hand to my forehead and then a cheek. "You're hot, but not feverish."

"It's probably just the flu. I didn't eat this morning and I feel rundown." I stared at the bag she set on the coffee table. "What's all that?"

Val flashed a proud smile. "It's the best friend Sick Starter Pack. Vegetable stew, ginger ale, sourdough bread fresh from the bakery, chocolate and bourbon. And a pregnancy test."

I groaned at her upbeat words and turned onto my side. "I'll take a double shot of bourbon, please and thank you."

"First the test," she insisted firmly. "And then food. After the test results, we can talk about the bourbon."

"Val." I'm not ashamed to say that I whined like a little girl. "I'm sick, not pregnant. I haven't had sex in ages until recently, and it wasn't even that long ago for this," I pointed at myself, "to be pregnancy symptoms."

Valona took a seat on the sliver of sofa beside me and laughed. "Do I need to remind you that it only takes one time to make a baby?"

"No, smartass."

She laughed again and gently rubbed my arm. "Then let me remind you that Gatlinburg was almost two months ago."

Two months. I sat up too fast and dropped back down just as quickly. "No, it can't be." Had it really been that long? "Can it?"

"It can, and it has been, so drink some water and take this to the bathroom."

I did as I was instructed, mostly to shut Valona up. I wasn't pregnant. I couldn't be. "It's your money to waste, but I really wish you wouldn't have."

"It's still a possibility, unless you've already gone through menopause?"

"I haven't," I sighed reluctantly. "But come on, Val. This is ridiculous. I'll be forty-one in a few months. I am not pregnant."

Valona pushed me towards the downstairs bathroom and shoved a bottle of water in my hand. "Then pee on the stick to ease my mind. When it tells you what you already seem to know, we'll gorge on chocolate and bourbon and you can tell me how ridiculous I can be. Deal?"

"Fine," I grumbled and closed the bathroom door, but once inside I didn't feel as confident as I had just a moment before. I stared at the offensive box for several long minutes. I couldn't be pregnant. What kind of forty year old woman got pregnant from a one night stand with her high school sweetheart? Not me. Definitely not me. To prove it, I chugged down the entire bottle of water and took both tests. I set the timer and joined Val in the living room. "Sourdough me, please."

"You gonna be all right, honey?"

"I'll be fine Val, because I'm not pregnant."

She laughed and shook her head like I was one of her twins. "Why are you sleeping with Ryan if you hate him?"

This was my best friend and if I could be honest with anyone, it was her. "Because I can't resist him. Some moments I feel like the old Pippa again, happy and carefree and so in love it was almost sickening. And then I remember how I felt watching him walk away, knowing it had never been real."

"And in those brief moments you end up naked?"

I nod. "Pretty much. It hasn't been planned, ever. It just sort of happened a few times."

"What's a few? Less than ten?"

"Yes."

She laughed. "More than five?"

"Maybe."

"I don't know Pippa, this sounds like explosive chemistry, maybe even love."

I shook my head at her words, because it might be chemistry, but it certainly wasn't love. I wouldn't let it be love, not ever again. "No matter what it sounds like, it's just a one time mistake that I keep repeating because the twenty year old girl in me can't let him go. That's all." Even I know that's a lie and I'm grateful to Valona for not calling me out.

"Whatever you need to tell yourself, honey. At least for the next three minutes or so." She smiled and I gave her a playful shove.

"What about you, any bad relationship decisions lately?"

"No," she sighed. "Nothing worth talking about."

Which meant there was something. "Tell me-,"

Valona jumped off the sofa like it was on fire just as the timer chimed from the bathroom. "Let's go."

I stood much slower than Val and let out a long breath. It was time to face the music, and hopefully not the music man.

CHAPTER 19

RYAN

"Holy hell man, it smells like armpit and whiskey in here." Roman stepped inside the recording studio, with our brother Derek trailing behind him. "Have you left here today?"

I shrugged at the matching shocked expressions on my brothers' faces and went back to the music sheet in front of me. "Not today. Or yesterday. Not for a while." Truth was, I hadn't left the studio except for short periods of sleep and bathroom breaks. I was in a fog, a fog of songwriting that seemed to never end. "I've hit a stride."

"Yeah?" Roman's worry transformed to excitement as he dropped down on the sofa at the far side of the room. "Anything good for me?"

"I got about six songs that I think are perfect for your

voice. The rest just depends on what you're going for. I think about eight are good for the band."

"You think?" Leave it to Derek to pick up on the details. "What's going on?"

"Nothing. I came down here last week because I had some chords I just couldn't get out of my head and then they just kept pouring out." I hadn't written like this in ages and it felt good, so damn good. At least my professional life was going much better than my nonexistent personal life. "Got more songs than I really need, I guess I'll have to sell 'em."

My brothers looked at each other and then back at me, their worried expressions returned. "What's going on?" Derek was almost annoyed.

"How was the tropical vacation with Sally?"

"Her name was Tally, and it was fine. Don't change the subject. What's going on with you?"

"Nothing. Just working on our next album, writing and stuff." The stuff being the thing that kept me locked in my studio for nearly fourteen straight days. "How was LA?"

Roman grinned. "Great. I mean I had to sit through a lot of meetings with executives and creatives going over the concept for the album, but the press was good. People are excited about my album and happy to know The Gregory Brothers are still going strong."

All caught up on their lives, Roman and Derek turned to me. "What?"

"If you're not gonna tell us what's wrong," Derek growled, "at least let us hear the music."

That I could do, happily. We listened to Roman's songs first and then the eight I'd earmarked for TGB. "I think we should just title the album TGB," I told them and then played the final three songs.

"Holy shit," Roman beamed. "You *have* been in the zone. These are incredible, Ry. Seriously fuckin' incredible."

"Thanks. I'm pretty proud of them." They were some of my best songs, period. The lyrics and music and composition were all perfect.

"Let's hear the rest," Derek urged, still staring at me like he thought I might be on the verge of a mental breakdown.

It took another two hours, but we listened to all the songs I'd come up with since the tour ended, and I hadn't realized just how many there were. "Didn't realize there were so many actually."

"I guess I don't need to ask if things are on again with you and Pippa," Derek guessed correctly. "Saw her at the Dark Horse and she is looking mighty damn fine." I glared at my brother but he just laughed, that knowing look in his eyes.

"There is no me and Pippa." I'd spent every free moment between writing and recording, trying to figure out what I could say to her to make things right and nothing came to me. Just songs.

Derek shook his head. "I don't know why you're wasting time with a restaurant. You're going to make a killing off all these songs and residuals."

"I just wanted something else to keep me busy when I wasn't obsessing about writing songs."

"Speaking of restaurants," Roman said and patted his belly dramatically. "I'm starving."

"You're always starving," I shot back in a familiar refrain.

"He's got a hollow leg," Derek added with a smile. "But I could eat too, and I'm eager to get an up close and personal look at Pippa. Roman said she's even hotter now."

I knew he was trying to get a rise out of me so I gave in to the urge and punched him in the shoulder. "Don't be stupid."

Roman shook his head. "Let's go. I hear you have a pretty little purple haired chef and you know how much I love quirky chicks."

We all piled into my truck and headed for Dark Horse. The parking lot was packed, and I had to double check the schedule Pippa shared with me but I rarely bothered to check. "I hope there's room for us."

Derek laughed. "You own the place."

"Yeah but this prime real estate is part of an events venue which means the restaurant is often booked out, or the special occasion rooms are full and, it's a whole thing that Pippa keeps track of." I hadn't seen her in weeks and she hadn't reached out either, which I didn't know how to feel about.

"I'll use my charm if being you being the boss doesn't work," Roman offered and hopped from the truck, full swagger on as he walked inside Dark Horse.

All eyes, of course, turned to us. The dining room grew quiet as we stepped up to the dark wood podium and waited like guests. Devon walked up with a frown on his face. "Hey Boss. Did I miss a reservation from you?"

"Nope. These knuckleheads showed up uninvited and begging to be fed. Any room for us?"

"Of course. Right this way."

"Nice suit," Roman said to Devon with a smile. "Think I could pull that off?"

"Absolutely. With that hair and the scruff, that's a magazine cover waiting to happen."

"Can I borrow him, Ry?"

"No," I growled and slid inside the round booth, searching the dining room for the woman I couldn't get out of my mind. "Where's Pippa?"

Devon frowned at me like I should know. "She's at home. Been fighting some bug on and off for the past few weeks, but when I saw her yesterday she looked much better." He flashed a nervous smile. "Don't worry, she's still been working like crazy to make sure all the scheduled events went off without a hitch. That's probably why she's still sick."

Pippa was sick. That's probably why she hadn't reached out to me. *Yeah, right.* It was a nice thought, but I realized that by not reaching out to her, my employee, I probably fell into the role of asshole. Again.

"All right. Good."

Roman and Derek ordered the sample platter for two, just so they could set eyes on Nina. "I already called dibs," Roman snarled. "So back off."

Derek held his hands up defensively. "How about we just let the lady decide?"

"Whatever," Roman growled and turned to me. "Real talk now big brother, what's going on with you and Pippa?"

"Nothing and that's the damn problem." I gave them an abbreviated version of my relationship with Pippa since returning to Carson Creek. "She won't let go of the past."

Derek waited until the first course was delivered before he spoke. "I always wondered why she didn't come with us to Nashville. I didn't realize you kicked her to the curb before then. I just figured she chose not to come."

My nostrils flared as anger surged in my blood. "I didn't kick her to the curb, dammit."

"You did," he insisted. "I was fully prepared to have Pippa with us every step of the way, between college classes. It was weird that she wasn't there."

"Totally weird," Roman agreed and popped the

appetizer in his mouth with a groan. "So damn good, but too damn small."

"She needed to live her life. Why am I the only one who understands that?"

Derek laughed. "Guess I see why she's not getting over the past. You still haven't apologized." He let out a low whistle. "How in the hell did you get her into bed again?"

"I'm irresistible," I growled. "Sexually, anyway."

"More Than Chemistry," Roman added on a knowing sigh. "That song, it's another Pippa classic I'm sure of it."

Derek nodded, a slow smile parted his lips. "Yep. Without a doubt."

Course after course, my brothers continued to dissect my relationship with Pippa and my songs about her. It was tiresome, but it also highlighted the fact that I hadn't gotten over her, that distance had done nothing to dull my feelings for her.

I sent Pippa two texts and she didn't respond to either, didn't even read them. "Can we talk about something else, please?"

"Sure. I wonder who will ask her out first," Derek mused. "My bet is on the bank president. He's new to town, has a good job and won't leave for months at a time."

Derek knew what he was doing and the effect it would have on me, and it worked, dammit. The thought of Pippa, *my* Pip, dating someone else didn't sit right with me. "She's not dating anyone, damn you."

Derek laughed.

"She will, bro. It's inevitable. She's smart and beautiful, and just a little bit wild. As soon as you get out of her way, she's going to date. A lot."

With just the dessert course left, I stood. "I have to go."

Derek passed a fifty dollar bill to Roman. "You won," he said with a surprised shake of his head. "I can't believe he made it through dinner."

"You bet on me?"

"Damn straight," Roman said with a proud smile and pocketed the fifty. "Thanks for the win, Ry. Go check on your woman."

"She's not my woman." Not yet. But she would be.

Soon.

CHAPTER 20
PIPPA

The pounding in the distance pulled me from a restless sleep, and I couldn't decide if I was happy about it or annoyed. I sat up and caught a wave of nausea that gave me my answer. I was annoyed. No, I wasn't just annoyed, I was angry. Sleep, no matter how terrible, was preferable than this nonstop sickness. The constant urge to empty my stomach whether I wanted to or not, was awful. It was completely unfair.

It was my punishment for being forty and acting like an eighteen year old when it came to sex. I mean, what self-respecting woman in this day and age didn't use protection? Worse, protection hadn't even occurred to me until Val showed up with that pregnancy test.

A silly ridiculous woman.

So sure, I would have an adorable baby in about

seven months, but the universe was determined to make this pregnancy hell right from the start.

And the damn pounding persisted. "Just a minute!" I yelled from the sofa and slowly pushed my way to a standing position. My legs wobbled for a brief moment before they strengthened enough for me to carry my angry behind to the front door and find out what idiot thought it was a good idea to invade a sick woman's sleep. "What the hell do you…Ryan?"

I hadn't seen him in weeks. Hadn't heard from him either, almost as if he had a sixth sense about the baby and had chosen to stay away. It wouldn't surprise me one bit.

Ryan looked even better than usual, his hair was messy and his facial hair was overgrown. He had that sexy mountain man look going, and it was irresistible. He shoved his hands deep into the pockets of his dark jeans and let out a shaky sigh.

"I heard you were sick and figured I'd check in on you."

"I'm fine," I insisted even though I knew exactly how I looked. "Just a little bug."

"Devon said you've been sick for weeks now."

Something he would know if he cared as much as he pretended to. "I have been, and I'm not really in the mood for visitors right now. Thanks for stopping by," I told him and closed the door.

He pushed it open before the door closed all the way

and glared at me. "I needed to see for myself that you were okay."

"I am perfectly all right, at least I was before someone interrupted the rest I desperately need in order to heal. Enjoy the rest of your evening, Ryan." I moved around him, careful not to touch him, and gripped the door handle with as much force as I could.

He refused to take the hint. "How long have you been sick?"

"That's not really any of your business. I'll be at work tomorrow if that's what you're worried about. I haven't been slacking, everything is taken care of." I folded my arms and glared at him, disappointed in myself for even believing he was really here to check on me.

"If that's what I'm...is that what you really think of me?"

"What else am I supposed to think? I told you that I'm fine, but you refuse to go away, which means you're worried about your investment. I've just assured you that your investment is fine. Everything is just perfect, so now you can go."

"I can't do that."

"Why not? It's what you do best."

He let out a low growl and shook his head with a dark look for me. "Give it a damn rest, would you Pip? I'm so tired of hearing that same old song you keep humming."

"Then leave. Go, and this will be the last time you ever have to hear that song again."

We had a staredown, right there in my front hall. His gaze was unyielding as it held mine. "Can't we get past this, Pip?"

"If you stop pushing for more than a boss-employee relationship, we would be fine."

"So that's it, then? You can just ignore the chemistry, the history, the fact that there's still something between us?"

"I have to, Ryan. You'll leave again in a few months for tour, so no matter how I feel, or how I *could* feel, you're not a good bet. You walked away once and this time, I know you'll do it again." And I knew he wouldn't ask me to come with him again either. It would ruin all the backstage fun the boys had on the road.

"So I have to give up my career?"

"No. I'm not asking you to do that. I'm not asking you for anything, I just answered your questions." I would have never asked him to give up his dream, his career for me, or for anyone else. "I'm happy you have the career you always wanted and I would never want to take that from you."

"I figured you resented my career. Have you listened to any of the songs?"

"Only a few, but that doesn't mean that I'm not proud of you guys for what you've achieved." Tears welled up behind my eyes and I tried to shake them away, but the burning sensation continued. And then the nausea returned. "Thank you for checking on me Ryan. That was nice of you." I tried to push him out the door but his big body wouldn't budge, so I took off at a full run, making it to the bathroom just in time.

Thank goodness.

CHAPTER 21
RYAN

Something was really wrong with Pippa. She wouldn't say so, but she had been sick for too long for just a simple bug. And the way she hauled ass to the bathroom left me more worried than she would probably like.

Instead of taking off like I was sure she wanted, I took a seat in the living room and waited.

And waited.

The sound of her retching echoed down the hall and I listened with barely a wince, my worry was so great. With no other sounds in the house, the noise sounded even louder, but still I waited, as she turned on the water and let it run for a few minutes.

Ten, maybe fifteen minutes later, Pippa emerged from the bathroom. Her bare footsteps were slow and tentative as she made her way towards me, she sucked in a startled gasp when she noticed I was still there. With a dark glare and a hand to her chest, she sighed tremulously.

"What are you still doing here?"

I took in the sight of her pale skin and the deep purple crescents under her eyes, and even though I was no doctor, you couldn't tell me something wasn't wrong with her.

"I'm worried about you, Pip. Did you really lose your job in Chicago or did you come home because you're sick?" It wouldn't be unheard of for terminally ill people to want to die at home, surrounded by friends and family.

She nodded and put her hands on her hips, her tone sarcastic when she spoke. "Yeah something *is* wrong with me, starting with my decision to return to Carson Creek." She looked at me like she didn't believe my concern was genuine.

"Can't I be worried about you, Pip?" I hated the constant antagonism between us. It made me feel powerless, because no one had ever hated me like this before.

Pippa stood tall, her posture a picture of defiance and anger. "I would rather you weren't worried, Ryan. This isn't the first time I've been sick in the past twenty years, and I *somehow* managed to take care of myself every single time. I'm an expert at taking care of myself."

That's because she didn't have anyone in Chicago

she could rely on to take care of her when she fell ill. She had done it all on her own, relying on no one, reaching out to no one for help. And the stubborn woman was determined to do the same now. "I can help."

"I don't need any help. I'm fine." Even the words sounded exhausted as they fell from her lips. She was pale and looked frail, like a strong gust of wind might knock her over.

"You're pale, Pip."

She gritted her teeth and glared at me so hard that if looks could kill, I would have been a dead man. "I know what I look like Ryan, and if you don't like it, feel free to leave. The door is that way."

I stood and took a step forward, angry that she was being so obstinate. "Dammit Pip, stop misreading everything I say. I'm worried that this is more than just a bug."

Her blue eyes were round and wide. For a moment I thought she might tell me what was really wrong with her, but stubborn as ever, Pip stayed silent.

Okay, she wouldn't make it easy on me but that didn't surprise me. It did however piss me off, and I raked one annoyed hand through my hair. "I just want to help you, Pip. Tell me what I can do."

She stared at me with watery blue eyes filled to the brim with wariness. She didn't trust me, not with anything more than her sexual pleasure. I thought for a second she might confide in me, might tell me what was wrong and how I could help. Instead she waved a hand towards the door with a sigh. "Just go. Please. I need to rest if I'm going to make it in to the office tomorrow."

Even getting those words out had been too much for her, which in turn, had been too much for me to witness. I closed the gap between us and folded Pip in my arms. She stiffened at first, and then leaned against me, allowing me to take her weight and in that moment I knew, without a doubt, that something bigger than a bug was wrong with her.

"I'll go, Pip. For now. But I will be back." I dropped a kiss on her forehead and took a step back.

"That isn't necessary, Ryan." The words came out in a whisper, showing just how exhausted and unwell she really was. All of her fight and fire were gone, in its place was just fatigue.

I wouldn't let her words stop me from watching out for her, taking care of her. Not anymore.

CHAPTER 22
PIPPA

There was nothing like a hot shower to wash away the ick and infuse my body with enough energy to make it through a quick breakfast of toast and butter, and hot tea. After breakfast I would slip into comfortable work clothes, touch up my makeup and head to Dark Horse with a smile that I didn't feel plastered on my face. That smile would remain in place for the remainder of my shift, until I could ensconce myself in my house and rest until morning.

Then I would do it all over again.

And again.

With my hair blow dried into soft waves and half of my makeup done, I froze at an unfamiliar sound coming from downstairs. I knew I was being silly, because this was Carson Creek, not Chicago. People didn't break into homes here, not in broad daylight anyway. I reached for the bat beside my bed and tiptoed down the steps, straining to hear what exactly the movement was. A burglar would find nothing of value in the kitchen aside from some purposefully mismatched dinnerware, high end appliances that came with the house, and a red stand mixer that was my pride and joy.

At the bottom of the steps I hefted the bat, ready to strike as I made my way to the kitchen. Standing in front of my stove, and looking good enough to eat in low slung jeans that hugged his backside and a well-worn gray t-shirt, was Ryan.

"What are you doing?" But I didn't need confirmation of his actions because the scents quickly overwhelmed me.

Ryan turned with a scowl and a silicon spatula in his hand. "I'm making breakfast. Devon said you were running yourself down, and I figured a nice big breakfast would help." He was so earnest, so genuine in his concern that I wanted to relax my shoulders and offer gratitude for his actions.

That's what I would have loved to do, and probably would have done in an alternate universe where the scent of greasy bacon, creamy butter and eggs, didn't create a trifecta of hell that made my stomach lurch and flip a few times.

"Well, dammit, who asked you to do any of that?" I motioned to all the food and all the dishes laid out on the counter and cluttered in the sink.

"Sorry sweetheart, I didn't hear ya. The words you're looking for are *thank you*."

"Thank you?" I sucked in a breath at his presumptuous words. I opened my mouth to give this man a big piece of my mind, but that inhale had been a little too energetic and the smells got in there, good and deep. Instead of words, a groan came out and I smacked one hand over my mouth. And then the other. My gaze zipped to the sink, but it was full of dishes so I turned away from Ryan and hightailed it to the bathroom where I emptied my stomach for the second time this morning.

There was nothing much left to spew up, so I spent long minutes retching until my stomach muscles ached from pushing up the gross yellow liquid that told me my stomach was well past empty.

Needless to say that my morning was not off to a good start.

My reflection was pale, but it had nothing to do with the unflattering fluorescent lighting. There were big bags under my eyes that layers of expensive concealer couldn't hide. I looked just as bad as I felt, which should have made me feel better, but it didn't. It would take a hell of a lot more makeup than I currently wore to make me look not half-dead and closer to normal.

I rinsed my mouth and splashed some cold water on my face, taking a deep breath before I opened the door and made my way to the living room. A small, hopeful part of me hoped that Ryan had been grossed out and left while I was in the bathroom. But I knew he would be there, somewhere. Waiting with his endless questions.

And there he was, arms folded over his chest, a brow arched in my direction. His expression was expectant, like I owed him an explanation for my sickness.

You do, my conscience niggled, but I shoved that silly, reckless voice down deep. Ryan didn't need to know anything, not yet. I glared right back at him, and for extra measure, pointed at him in accusation. "How did you get into my house?"

He sat there, as cool as you please, and nodded. "You left the door open. You shouldn't really do that Pip, anybody could just walk right in."

"Newsflash, Ryan. Anybody did."

He let out a low, amused chuckle at my words.

I rolled my eyes, ignoring the way the deep, rich sound rolled over me like a warm blanket. "Thanks for breakfast, but I'm not in the mood. You can go now, I'm fine and I need to get ready for work." I needed even more time to look healthy enough that my coworkers wouldn't pepper me with unnecessary questions.

"Pippa," he growled. "Listen to me. You can't go into work like this."

"Why not? I'm not contagious."

He got up from the sofa with a frown. "So you know what's wrong with you?"

"Of course I do, dammit. I am a grown woman."

His shoulders fell in relief, but Ryan wasn't done. Not yet. "And?"

"And what, Ryan?"

"Just tell me, Pippa."

His pleading nearly got to me, but I wasn't ready to confide in him what had become of our reckless, ill-advised nights together. Not yet, not until I had a clear plan for how I would handle single motherhood on my own. "I told you that it's just a bug and if you don't get out of here, I'm going to be late for work."

"Dammit woman, just tell me what the hell is wrong with you! Are you dying?"

Some days I felt like I was, but the feeling usually passed. Eventually. "No, I am not dying. I'm generally healthy, just a little under the weather." And according to the doctor I would continue to feel under the weather for another few weeks. Or the next seven months. "Just leave Ryan. Please."

"Not until you tell me what's wrong with you." Under different circumstances I might have found his pushiness endearing. I might have even confused his desire to know with a sincere desire to know. But I knew better.

"It's none of your damn business, Ryan!"

"I have a right to know, Pippa. If you're too sick to work, I might have to find a replacement manager until you're well again."

I sucked in a breath, careful not to take in any of the

smells that still lingered in the air. "Are you threatening my job?"

"No, I just think that as your boss, I should know if you have a major illness."

Pregnancy wasn't a major illness, was it? But his question made me laugh bitterly. "Being my boss is exactly why you have no right to ask about my health. Just because we had sex a few times doesn't entitle you to the intimate details of my life." At least not until I decided to share those details with him.

Ryan shrugged nonchalantly. "I could just hire a PI to find out if you won't tell me."

Oh, that was it. He'd really pissed me off now. "The real Ryan Gregory has finally entered the room," I sneered at him. "Using your money to threaten me? Low." But it made it much easier to keep my news to myself. I marched towards the front door and yanked the door open, Ryan followed on my heels. "Go."

"In a minute." Arms folded, he stared down at me as if that slightly intimidating look would get me to reveal something I hadn't fully come to terms with yet. "Tell me what's wrong with you."

He didn't want to know and I knew that, but his highhandedness really got under my skin. "You want to know what's wrong with me, Ryan?"

"Yeah, I do. I need to know."

"Fine." I flashed a slightly wicked smile and pushed at his chest until he was on the other side of the doorway. "I'm pregnant, Ryan. That's what's wrong with me. So you see it's not contagious or anything to worry about. I can still do my job and I'm not dying. Happy now?"

I could tell my words had shocked him, in large part due to the perfect imitation he was doing of a guppy fish, mouth opening and closing, a dumbfounded expression on his face. Ryan's hands moved from hanging at his sides to hooking his thumbs through his beltloops, but his expression never changed. It wasn't happy and it wasn't sad or angry.

It was blank.

I just told the man I'd been sleeping with for the past few months that I was pregnant, and his expression was...nothing. Hell, it was less than nothing.

It stung and I felt a fire of humiliation bloom in my chest, but I felt proud because Ryan's reaction didn't really surprise me. In fact, it was just what I expected. "That's what I thought. *Now*, you can leave."

Finally, he came back to life. Sort of. His mouth did that guppy thing again, but no words ever came out. Eventually he gave up, nodded distractedly and turned away from me before he made his way across our two yards and into his house. In utter and absolute silence.

I shouldn't have been mad, and I didn't even know why I was mad. All I knew was that anger roared through my veins and I stepped back inside my house and slammed the door as hard as I possibly could.

Now that I had Ryan's reaction to the news of my pregnancy, I could push away all thoughts of him and focus on what I had to do next. First, I needed to finish getting ready for work. Then, I would figure out if this house was right for me and a baby, or if I needed to start looking for something else. I probably needed to start looking, it wouldn't be fair to my kid to force them to live in a house beside a man who didn't want them.

There was a lot to do and not enough time in a day to do it all, or even think of it all.

I would make time, I promised myself, as soon as this dang morning sickness went on about its way and left me the hell alone.

Just like the man responsible for the morning sickness had done.

CHAPTER 23
RYAN

Pregnant.

Pippa was pregnant, and even now, days later, there was no way to stop my mind from spinning like a tornado. I hadn't been able to write, to think, to record anything since I walked away from Pippa on wooden legs in a fog. Mind full of everything and nothing all at once.

Pregnant. It was unbelievable that she was pregnant. Weren't we too damn old for things like accidental pregnancies?

Apparently not.

Holy hell, I was going to be a father. I was going to be responsible for someone else's life, well-being and happiness. Truth be told, I didn't know how I felt about that. I hadn't actually thought about having kids because I hadn't been serious about anyone since Pippa, not even my ex-wife. We hadn't been together long enough to consider having children, and we hadn't known each other well enough to even have the kids talk before we got married.

Hell, I still didn't know how my ex felt about kids. Or Pippa. Or how I felt about having kids. Did I even want to be a father? A man doesn't get to my age without having kids if he truly wanted them. Right?

But the thought of having kids with Pippa wasn't just your run-of-the-mill thought of having kids in general. This wasn't general at all, this was Pippa, the love of my life. The woman I've wanted for nearly as long as I've drawn breath. Kids with Pippa had always been *the* dream, even when I walked away from her and she pretended as if I never existed. She was the woman for me and now she was having my baby.

All should be right in my world.

But all wasn't right, because we hadn't talked about having a baby together, and as far as I could tell, Pippa had only told me because she wanted to get rid of me. Because she assumed I would hear the news and I would run.

Which I did.

"I need to talk to someone." I knew that much was true, but I couldn't go to Lacey because she'd already warned me off of Pippa, and she'd be all kinds of upset before she got around to being happy about it. Roman and Derek couldn't see clearly because our relationship had produced some of the best songs I had ever written, and because Pippa was like a sister to them. There was no one else I trusted enough to have such an important conversation with, so I grabbed my keys and my guitar, hopped in my truck and drove. I drove for hours and hours, not even seeing the gorgeous Tennessee landscape as it passed me by.

I drove until I could make sense of Pippa's words, but I couldn't make heads or tails of anything beyond the fact that she was pregnant. So, I kept driving.

Pippa was pregnant with my baby. "You just had to push, didn't you?" My reflection had no sympathy for me for pushing when it was clear she wasn't ready to share the news with me. But the fact that Pippa didn't want to tell me, made me question if the child was mine at all. Maybe she'd just said it to get me to go away, to stop bothering her.

Yeah and maybe pigs would sprout wings and take flight among the birds.

The truth was, she told me because she was sure that it was the one thing guaranteed to get me to walk away. To leave her, again. And dammit, she was right, because here I was, hundreds of miles from Carson Creek instead of sitting with Pippa and planning for our child.

For our future.

I didn't know where I was, couldn't even find a sign to tell me what town or highway I was on, so I pulled over and reached for my guitar. Lyrics and music came in fits and starts, but somehow I managed to fill a small notebook and dozens of napkins with lyrics and music. I don't know how long I stayed on the side of the road, cars and eighteen wheelers whizzing by while I strummed and hummed until I had the skeleton of two new songs recorded on one of those recorder apps. I used them when it was necessary, but I would never get used to the idea of recording a song on my phone.

Before I knew it, the inside of my truck had cooled considerably and I realized the sun had gone down and darkness had settled all around me. I yanked a flannel from the back seat, tugged it on and went in search of sustenance, which led me to an all-night roadside diner.

"What'll it be honey?" The woman looked right out of central casting with a beehive hairstyle, a fifties style pink uniform and comfortable off-white orthopedic shoes to complete the picture. There was something comforting in that, and I smiled as she tapped her pen on the notepad.

"I'll have a large bowl of chili, a double cheeseburger with bacon, onion rings and a tall cola with no ice, thanks."

"Big appetite for a not so big man. Woman troubles?"

I laughed at her accurate guess. "That obvious?"

"When a guy like you is eating this much, either you lost your job or have woman troubles. Too handsome to have a nine to five, so woman is my guess. Want a milkshake? The chocolate one is made with real chocolate."

"How can I resist?"

"You can't honey, that's why I asked. Order'll be up in fifteen."

"Thanks." I smiled at her retreating form and shook my head, wondering what Pippa was up to at this exact moment. She hadn't called or reached out by any means, and truthfully I didn't expect her to. It was on me to call and check in with her, but I didn't because I'm a coward.

No you're not.

Except I was. I didn't want to call and face more rejection, not until I had my head on straight. Not until I knew exactly what to say to Pippa that wouldn't anger her further. I had to get it right this time.

So I rewrote the lyrics in a new notebook I'd bought at the gas station beside the diner while I waited for my food. When the food arrived, I ate like a man who hadn't eaten a real meal in weeks, maybe months. A big ol' slab of apple pie with melted cheddar on top, then I was full and ready to lay my head someplace quiet and anonymous.

I found a cheap hotel to get a decent night of rest, with the plan to return to Carson Creek in the morning, but when morning came I wasn't ready to face my life yet. Or the truth of what waited for me when I returned. So instead of heading back the way I came, I filled up my tank and kept driving heading to god knows where.

I drove until I was too exhausted and too lost to keep going, which kind of summed up my life lately. I found another anonymous place to rest, except sleep didn't come at all the second night. Or the third, or even the fourth dammit. No matter how long or how far I drove, no clarity came.

No answers came.

No plans magically formed in my mind.

Sometime after lunch a week later, hell maybe it was more than a week. I'd been driving, thinking and overthinking so long I had no idea how long I'd been gone, but I decided to head back home after a giant platter of ribs, macaroni and cheese, green beans and buttery biscuits. I took my time getting there, hoping I'd have answers before I stuck my key in the front door of my house.

CHAPTER 24
PIPPA

"Oh my goodness, what did he say." Val's eyes were wide with excitement as I sat beside her on the living room sofa and told her all about that early morning argument with Ryan where I blurted out the news of my pregnancy.

I shrugged. "He didn't say anything." That part still stung, but with each passing day, it was a pill that grew easier to swallow. This was Ryan, the guy who ran away from his problems rather than face them. It hurt like hell, but it was no surprise.

Val rolled her eyes and sipped her tea. "Oh, come on. What did he say, really?"

"Val," I sighed and shook my head. "He said nothing. Literally, nothing." I could close my eyes and see him as clear as day. The guppy fish impersonation, the dumbfounded expression on his face, all of it, and it made me angry all over again. "He said nothing. No words. Hooked his thumbs through his belt loops and walked away. That was a week ago."

"Wow. That's nuts."

My sentiments exactly, but I knew Val would read too much into that, so I laughed bitterly and paired it with a sardonic smile. "Had I known that would get rid of him so swiftly, I would have lied about being pregnant before things ever got this far."

"You wouldn't have, because you're a chicken and you would never risk that he might stick around and offer to take care of the baby."

"Ha! With all the evidence to the contrary?" I shook my head. "Ryan is who he is and I refuse to redefine it because it would make all of this easier. "It worked to get rid of him pretty damn quickly, that's for sure." And as glad as I was that he'd left me alone, part of me was sad—for my baby—that he'd walked away so easily. Again. I knew that kind of rejection and the pain it caused. It was the kind of pain that made you second guess every emotion, every relationship in your life. The mistrust ran deep and it was impossible to simply *will* oneself to trust again. "Now I just have to figure out how to be a forty year old single working mother." Should be easy, right?

Yeah, right.

Val stared at me, dark brows arched. "If I can manage it, so can you."

I nodded, appreciating her confidence. "No offense, but it's not the same. You had help when your girls were small. I can't afford to take three months off work to spend time with a baby, to bond with him or her. Even with what's left of my savings, time off and hospital bills will put a big dent in that number."

"Okay, I'll give you that, but you'll have something I didn't have. Me and my support." Val laid a hand on top of mine and gave it a supportive squeeze.

"I appreciate that, but Val, this is your time to get your business off the ground, to live your life. Not to mention, you have a fairly energetic pair of twins on your hands. You have no room in our life for the kind of baggage I'm packing these days."

"I can help you with a nanny since the one thing Rodney did do, was leave me with a ton of money."

"You're sweet for offering," I told her because borrowing money was the fastest way to ruin a friendship. "But I have to be able to do this on my own, and I don't even know how I'm going to do that. Healthcare costs associated with just having the baby might bankrupt me, and if it doesn't, childcare costs damn well will." I felt myself starting to spiral as all the things I needed to do before the baby arrived were tallied up in my head. The baby didn't have a room yet, or diapers, or onesies, or even a car seat. I can't bring a baby home from the hospital without a car seat. Can I? "I'm not sure I can do this, Val."

"Of course you can. You left Carson Creek and spent the past couple decades bossing around snooty waitresses, bullheaded chefs and placating people with more money than good sense. You can do this in your sleep."

I laughed. "Thanks for the vote of confidence, but I'm not so sure. You can't just yell at a baby to get his or her shit together, can you?"

"No," she laughed. "But you can find ways to convey that message without the profanity. Kids are sponges, that's lesson number one. Whatever you say will be repeated at daycare and kindergarten and all of the most inappropriate places you can imagine."

"That actually sounds pretty damn adorable. Promise I'll have a potty mouthed baby?"

"Knowing you, Pippa, I can just about guarantee it."

"Thanks, babe." I leaned over and gave my best friend a clumsy hug, nearly knocking over two mugs of tea in the process. "I needed that and I'm going to hold you to it."

Valona groaned. "I had a feeling you might say that. Now I have to come over every day and swear up a storm as the baby grows in your belly." She stroked her chin. "Okay, totally doable. You can count on me."

We shared another hug that was interrupted by the sound of a fist pounding on the front door, startling us both. I pulled back with wide eyes. "Angry lover looking for revenge?"

Valona laughed. "More like upset groupies hunting for you."

"Dammit, that's a good point. If it's for me, tell them I left town. Headed back to Chicago to become a professional modern dancer."

"Anything for you." Valona unfolded her long, svelte frame off the sofa and made her way towards the insistent knocking on the front door.

I held my breath as the seconds ticked by and I waited for Val's return, sure it would be an angry Ryan ready to give me a piece of his mind. The first I heard was footsteps, more than two sets and I sat a little taller and waited for the guests to enter the living room.

It wasn't Ryan, but the rest of his siblings. Lacey, Derek and Roman stepped in behind Valona, matching expressions of worry on each of their faces.

"Pippa," Lacey sighed. "Have you seen or spoken to Ryan?"

"No." Not since he walked away after learning we made a baby in Gatlinburg. I ignored the worry that built up in my stomach at their concerned expressions. It wasn't like Ryan to run without telling someone, then again, that was the Ryan I knew a lifetime ago.

Derek raked both hands through his hair and shook his head. "No one has seen or heard from him in more than a week." He looked at me suspiciously, like maybe I had his brother tied to a radiator in my basement.

"You're not the only one," I assured them as sincerely as I could.

"Why would he run off like this?" Roman asked the question to no one in particular, but it didn't take a genius to figure out why they'd shown up at Val's place. They figured his absence had something to do with me. "He's the level headed one of us."

Three sets of blue eyes landed on me and I stared back at them, remembering a time when Ryan's hazel eyes had caused him to question if he was part of the Gregory family for real. I helped him figure out that those hazel eyes belonged to his paternal grandmother, they were an odd gift of sorts.

Val turned to me too, silently urging me to tell them the truth, to give the Gregory siblings some sort of relief to ease their minds, but I didn't want to, and gave a subtle shake of my head.

I wasn't ready to share my news with anyone, let alone all of Ryan's siblings since they clearly blamed me for his out of character behavior. This was my secret to hold on to for as long as I could so I could make plans without the whole town giving me their input. But no one could look into those worried faces and let their anguish continue.

"Oh fine. He left again, I'm guessing, because I told him that I was pregnant."

Just as I suspected, a cold silence settled in Val's living room and they all continued to stare at me, faces showing off varying degrees of shock and anger and distrust. "That can't be right," Lacey insisted impatiently. "That kind of news wouldn't send him packing."

I sighed and pushed down the instinctive smart ass comment that was perched on the tip of my tongue. "I'm just telling you what you wanted to know. The last time I saw him or spoke to him was eight days ago when I told him that I was pregnant, and he walked away without one damn word." Again.

"But..." Roman began what I assumed would be an energetic defense of his brother, but even he was at a loss for words at the news.

"He must have been shocked," Derek said on a sigh, aggravated by his helplessness.

I held up my hands to stop whatever any of them might say next. "No offense, but I'm not interested in hearing you defend your brother's behavior because there is no defense. That was the last time I saw him or heard from him. I didn't even realize he was missing." Sure I noticed that the lights hadn't been on in days, but I figured he decided to shack up with someone else who had a better handle on proper birth control.

"Have you tried to reach out to him?" I didn't appreciate the accusation woven through Lacey's question.

"Nope." I did that once before, calling him nonstop after he broke up with me and left for Nashville, sure it was a joke or a mistake. Ryan hadn't picked up the phone, not even once, and I called it a lesson learned. When someone said you weren't enough, believe them.

Derek shook his head and sighed as he dropped down on Val's dainty damask chair. "I don't know why you wouldn't call. He was obviously in shock."

I let out a bitter laugh. "Unlike me? The middle-aged woman who actually has to carry this child? Who might end up without a job because she was stupid enough to...never mind." I sucked in a deep breath and held it for as long as I could before I let it out. "Ryan knew what he was doing when he left. He did it once before, so please, spare me the sainted Ryan spiel. If you want to find him, then I suggest you stop blaming me and go look for him."

"That's not what we meant to imply," Lacey began in a hurried tone. "Please, Pippa, we're just worried."

"I know that, and I get it. If he was my brother, I would be worried too. But he's your problem, and the fact that he ran from what he perceived to be a problem is on him. Not me." I turned to Val with a smile. "Thanks for listening today. I'll see you later." I reached out to her and hugged her tight before I grabbed my purse and rushed out the door and away from the Gregory family.

Derek had caught up to me by the time I made it to the curb where I'd parked and touched my arm. "I'm sorry, Pip. I know this isn't your fault."

I shrugged. "I know it's not, but thanks for saying so," I told him sarcastically.

"What if he's hurt somewhere?"

"What if he's just off doing whatever he does when he's not with you guys?"

"Lately that's been you from what I hear." Derek's cheeks flushed. "That's not what I meant."

I knew exactly what he meant. "Look Derek, I know you guys are worried and I am sorry for that, but I don't know your brother anymore. Hell, I'm not sure I ever knew him. But I definitely don't know where he would go or what he would do after receiving bad news. If I did, I would tell you."

"Bad news?" He shook his head. "You really got things backwards if that's what you think."

"No, that's what I know Derek. Don't try to paint me some pretty picture about his intentions. His actions speak loud and clear." Ryan wasn't just ignoring me, he'd left. Again.

The fact that I was right all along should have made me feel better, smug about being able to read my future, but it didn't. It made me feel rejected and not enough all over again.

"He'll be back," Derek insisted.

I shrugged off his words. "Maybe. Maybe not." I wouldn't hold my breath waiting either way.

I was older now and at least a little bit wiser, and I knew how to handle grief and rejection. I would take a day or two to feel my emotions and then I would move on because the one thing I knew without a doubt, was that life went on whether you were an active participant or a sulking bystander.

I planned to participate in the next stage of my life. Actively instead of reactively. That started with putting thoughts of Ryan Gregory squarely in my rearview mirror.

Where he and our sordid past belonged.

It might not have come about from the most ideal circumstances or with the right person, but I had always wanted a child of my own, and soon I would have that.

"He'll be back," Derek said again, his tone firm and insistent as it broke through my own musings on the man I couldn't seem to stay away from.

"See you around Derek." Two days to sulk and to cry. Two days to regret returning to the arms of a man who'd already rejected me. Two days of eating my emotions and then I would figure out how to map out my life as a single mother.

Because no matter what, life goes on.

CHAPTER 25

RYAN

"Hey Pippa, when you get a minute we should talk."

I popped my head into the manager's office the morning I returned to town, looking like hell and feeling like a fool.

Pippa looked up from the computer screen with first a startled, and then a bored expression before she nodded. "I need to update the schedules for the week and reach out to our alcohol vendors, and then I have to check in with Margot about the upcoming events. There are six over the next two weeks."

It was a blow off if I'd ever heard one, but I was her boss and Pippa, bless her heart, was trying to be polite. "That's the priority, but we need to talk."

Finally, she gave me her full attention. Arms folded,

she leaned against the back of the chair and sighed. "What is it?"

I looked over my shoulder to make sure there were no hungry ears looking for a morsel of gossip and stepped inside. "You're pregnant."

"Correct." Her hands were folded on top of the desk, still as a stone, her gaze immovable.

"And I'm the father?"

There it went, just a flash of emotion and it was gone as quickly as it had come. "I'm not doing this with you right now. I'm trying to get some work done before the dinner rush starts Ryan, so please, just let me do my job."

Shit, she was right. I couldn't use my position as owner to bully her into having a personal conversation on the clock. It was a bad look, and if it were anyone other than Pippa, it would be a recipe for a lawsuit.

"All right. I'm sorry to bother you." I turned away and nearly smacked into Devon.

His brows dipped into a concerned frown. "You all right, Boss? You seem out of it."

I laughed at his phrase. "You mean since I vanished for almost two weeks? Yeah, I'm fine. Mostly. I think. Hell, I don't know."

"That was about as clear as mud. Wanna talk about it?"

"Yes. No. Honestly, I don't even know what to talk about, or how to begin talking about it."

Devon nodded sagely. "Does it have anything to do with Pippa's ongoing bug and frequent trips to the bathroom? The way she holds her breath in the kitchen or breathes through her mouth when she thinks no one is paying attention?"

I frowned, because I didn't know what the hell any of that meant.

Devon let out a low, half-amused laugh. "Morning sickness, Ryan."

Oh. Right. "Yeah then, I guess maybe it does." I looked back at the closed door and shook my head. "Thanks for the offer, but I think I'd better talk to her before I talk to anyone else."

"I'm here if you want to talk, but it seems to me as if your brothers and sister already know."

"What? How?"

Devon flashed a sympathetic smile that made me feel like a pathetic old man. "You should talk to them. After you talk to Pippa." Devon gave my shoulder a supportive squeeze and then walked away, leaving me alone with my thoughts which was a bad place to be.

I waited around all shift, chatting with customers who seemed to appreciate having an aging rock star pour their wine, catching up with people around town who dropped in for a steak and a beer, all the while just waiting for Pippa to give me the time of day. All through the closing procedures, she ran around checking and double checking every little detail before allowing servers, busboys, the bartender and kitchen staff leave for the night.

The restaurant had been empty for twenty minutes and still there was no sign of Pippa, and my efforts to respect her need for space went out the window. I unlocked the front door and went in search of the woman, promising myself I would give her a good talking to if she'd exited from the back door in an effort to avoid me. But I came to a stop just inside her office when I found her head resting on folded arms. She was sound asleep.

"Stubborn woman," I grumbled and went around the desk to shut her laptop and gather her in my arms. If I let her, she would run herself into the ground out of spite alone.

She stirred in my arms while I locked up the restaurant and pushed at my chest. "What in the hell do you think you're doing?"

"I'm driving you home."

"I can drive myself and I walked to work today."

I balked at her words. "Are you out of your damn mind, woman? It's late as hell, even in a small town that's too late to walk home on your own." Despite her sleepy, uncoordinated movements, I managed to get Pippa settled in the passenger seat with the belt locked at her hip. "You're so exhausted you'd fall over before The Old Country House was out of sight." I slammed the door and jogged around to the driver's side with a smile because she was too tired to fight me.

"Yeah, I'm exhausted, but I haven't lost all my senses," she growled in my direction as I fired up the engine. "And the last thing I want or need is for you to carry me around like some stupid cave man."

"Some might just see it as a man concerned about a woman he's known his whole life, a pregnant woman working more hours than she should, I might add."

She folded her arms and jutted her chin out defensively. "I work as long as needed to get the job done."

"Well maybe I'll have to force you to cut back."

"Don't even think of interfering in my job that way, Ryan. I mean it."

I smiled at the sound of Pippa all riled up.

"What's so damn funny?"

"You," I answered and turned off the engine in front of her house. "You're still sexy as hell when you're fired up, angry and ready to argue." Before she could say another word, I jumped from the truck and went around to grab her in my arms.

"Don't say that and put me down, damn you." She didn't fight me on the walk up to the front door, just shoved the key in the lock and turned, allowing me to set her on the sofa.

"Why shouldn't I say that? Nobody is sexier than you when you're upset."

Pippa let out an exhausted sigh and let herself sink

into the sofa, propping her feet up on the coffee table. "Whatever, Ryan. You don't have to stay, I'm tired and going to bed so you can...go."

"What if I want to stay?"

She let out a huff of laughter that was far from amused. "I don't need you to stay here out of guilt, Ryan. There's nothing to feel guilty about, so please, just leave me alone."

"We need to talk Pip."

She nodded. "I know you didn't plan for this, but guess what? I didn't plan for this either, but it's now *my* reality and I'm fine with it. I'm happy about it, in fact." She sat a little taller but her exhaustion wouldn't allow it for too long.

I heard what she was saying, and I didn't like it one bit, so I glared down at her. "I'm hearing a whole of I's and me's, but that's my child too Pippa."

"Oh," she arched a brow up at me. "Now you're sure of that?"

"It was just a damn question, Pip."

"Yeah and it was an insulting one." She raised her hands to stop the apology on the tip of my tongue. "Look, it doesn't matter Ryan. If you want to be involved with the baby, do it. I'm not trying to tie you down to a life you don't want, but I also don't want you to make promises you don't intend to keep."

I turned my head to the ceiling, arms outstretched as frustration coursed through my veins as I let out a low, growl. "Back to this again? How many times do we have to go through this same old argument, Pip?"

"We don't have to have any arguments at all Ryan. I asked you to leave." Her eyes fluttered shut and her head fell back against the sofa cushion. She was silent for so long I thought maybe she'd drifted off to sleep. "I can only go by what I know of our past, Ryan and back then you lied to me often."

"I did not! I never lied to you, not once."

She nodded. "Every time you said you could see me in a white dress with my cleavage spilling over, our redheaded kids with your exact shade of hazel eyes, it was a lie. Every time you told me you saw us holding hands, all wrinkled and gray haired as we rocked together on the porch sipping Tennessee lemonade, you lied to me. You knew long before I did that we didn't have a future, but still you let me believe. No, you didn't just let me believe it, you sold me on a dream you knew would never come true." She released another tired sigh. "If those aren't broken promises, then I don't know what qualifies in your book."

I had no response, because I could see exactly how that was her perspective, but it wasn't true. "I loved you Pip, more than anyone before or since. I *did* see that future for us, every time I said it, I saw it. I thought that was what lay ahead for us."

"You didn't. You'd already planned your move, and you knew long before I did that I wasn't coming with, wasn't even invited. So when and how were we going to have that future?"

Shit. She was absolutely right. I did want that future, and every night I saw it as clearly as I saw me and my brothers on stage performing for large crowds. But I hadn't thought about how both of those dreams were going to come true.

Pippa kicked off her shoes and turned to let her whole body sink into the sofa. "I'm not trying to hurt you Ryan, but I have a plan and I can do this without you if that's what you prefer. But you've given me no reason to trust you or your word. So please just think long and hard about what you want, what you *really* see in your future, before making promises."

"I have done nothing but think about this since you said those words to me, Pip. All I've done is think about the fact that I'm going to be a father, and I'll be doing it with a woman who hates me."

"I don't hate you, Ryan. I just can't trust you the way you want me to. But I trust that my job is safe as long as I'm performing well."

"Of course your job is safe. You've made Dark Horse succeed far more than I could have imagined. Your job is safe, unless you put your health and the baby's health at risk."

"That's for me to decide," she shot back around a yawn.

"I'm sorry Pip."

"What for?"

I smiled even though she couldn't see me because it was such a typical Pippa question. "Because you're right. I loved you to the moon and back as a teenager, and the truth is that I never stopped. You're just it for me, Pip. But I didn't think about how I could have success with the band and with you, and I thought it was selfish to ask you to come to Nashville with us when you had plans to work restaurants in New York and Chicago, San Francisco. You wanted to do it all and see it all, and I wanted that for you, that and so much more." I shook my head, and what an idiot I'd been for so long. Too long. "I should have just talked to you. I don't know why I didn't, we talked about everything back then, nothing was too big or too small for us to talk about for hours. It's some of my best memories of us. But I didn't, and it messed everything up."

I sat back in the comfortable striped chair that faced the short end of the coffee table and waited for her to absorb what I'd said, to gather her own thoughts, and respond.

Except all I got was a soft snore accompanied by even breathing. She'd fallen asleep. I'd poured my heart out—finally—and she'd missed it all due to exhaustion.

Which meant I had to find a way to say those words to her all over again, and I knew just how to do it. I dropped a quick kiss on her forehead, locked the door and made my way home.

CHAPTER 26
PIPPA

"Hey Devon, why is the stage set up? I don't have anything on my schedule." The past week had been busy with the event rooms in the restaurant booked every single night, and I was so tired I slept on the couch, fully dressed until morning.

Devon turned with a grin. "Live performance. Impromptu."

"Oh. Okay." As long as it wasn't some big event that infringed on the schedule, I could handle it. "Who is it? I'll start doing some social media blasts to get more butts in the seats."

"It's a surprise," he said cryptically. "For everyone."

"Everyone except you?"

He shrugged. "I'm special that way."

"Well today is my day off technically, so I'm going to

finish up some paperwork and then Val's meeting me here for an early dinner." Early because I couldn't seem to keep my eyes open past nine-thirty when I wasn't at the restaurant, and because she had an early shoot in the morning.

"Valona reserved a table."

My brows dipped in confusion. "She did? When?"

Devon shrugged. "Don't know, all I know is there's a table reserved under her name for today. Six o'clock."

"Okay." I made my way back towards the peace and quiet of my office, away from the sights and sounds and smells of the restaurant that still weren't particularly easy on my stomach. But managing a restaurant was more than a full-time job, and staying on top of paperwork took up most of my time.

***

A knock sounded on the door and startled me. "Yeah?"

The door opened and Val stood there dressed in a long flowing black skirt with a matching shirt, a multi-colored scarf belt around her waist. "Did you forget about dinner?"

"What? No way. It's only three o'clock, Val. I didn't forget."

Her lips pulled into a sympathetic grin and she pointed to the big clock on the wall. "It's five minutes after six, Pippa. You must have fallen asleep."

I glanced at the clock on the computer screen and

sighed. "Must have. Give me two minutes to save this and wash my face and I'll meet you in the dining room. Promise."

"I've already ordered a whiskey with a beer chaser. You're the designated driver tonight pregnant lady."

"Pregnant lady reporting for duty," I shot back with a salute and a smile.

Five minutes later I was seated across from my best friend and feeling good. Not just, *not sick*, but actually good. Tired, but I had a smile on my face and I felt genuinely hungry as I ordered a roasted tomato bisque appetizer, and crab risotto. Valona arched her brows in surprise. "This is a change of pace. You look as if you're back in the land of the living."

I rolled my eyes and smiled. "Thanks, I think. You picked a good night, according to Devon there's live music tonight."

"Oh goody! How are things going with Ryan?"

"They aren't." He hadn't been around much since the night he drove me home from the restaurant and poured his heart out to me while I pretended to be asleep. It was a crap thing to do and I knew it, but my heart needed to be protected from a man who could shatter it. "I haven't seen much of him since he returned to town."

Valona's eyes narrowed to slits as she eyed me suspiciously. "Why don't I believe you?"

"Because you are a suspicious, cynical sort. You

should really work on believing in humanity more," I joked.

"I'm not talking about humanity, I'm talking about you, my best friend in the whole wide world. What aren't you telling me?"

I rolled my eyes and let out a put upon sigh. "I'm not telling you that Ryan poured his heart out to me and that I pretended to be asleep because it's easier to hate him, to mistrust him, than it is to risk letting him break my heart all over again. Mine and the baby's."

"Whoa." Valona sank back against her chair and whistled. "That's a lot."

"I know. Am I a horrible person?"

Valona shrugged as the low strains of a bluesy rock song started. Two different guitars played the same eight notes on repeat until a set of drums kicked in followed by a keyboard.

"Possibly," she joked and took a sip of beer.

"Gee thanks."

The music grew louder and ended our conversation, and I forced my attention away from the bisque and towards the stage. I gasped at the sight of The Gregory Brothers on stage and turned to Valona with a question in my eyes.

"Did you know they were performing?"

My best friend, the traitor, shrugged. "Listen to the song, Pip."

I turned away from the stage because I couldn't look

at him, not if this was what I thought it was, and listened while I sipped the now tasteless bisque.

"Good evening ladies and gentlemen. Thank you for coming out to the Dark Horse, and thanks for letting me crash your dinner this evening." Ryan spoke to the crowd and I turned back around because usually Roman was the front man with his big personality and charisma. "This is a new song I wrote and, well, I think the words speak for themselves. Enjoy."

The guitar sound dominated the song but not as much as Ryan's deep, smooth voice as he sang of apologies and forgiveness.

My whole world
My everything
She was everything to me
And for all the harm I did, I owe her an apology

The chorus repeated, almost as if on purpose, to make sure that I couldn't forget them.

I'm sorry, baby
So damn sorry
I wasn't man enough to tell you the truth
I'm sorry, baby
So damn sorry
I couldn't be there for you

The lyrics were heartfelt and they went straight from Ryan's lips and pierced my heart. Everyone was right, he was a talented song writer, because the lyrics brought tears to my eyes.

Can you forgive me?
Can I make up for the past?
Can I undo the hurt and the pain I caused
To get back the greatest love I ever had?

By the time the song ended, I was a bawling mess. Tears streamed down my cheeks and I gasped and hiccoughed as I fought for oxygen. It wasn't pretty, not nearly as beautiful as that song.

"Holy hell, that was great, wasn't it?"

Val nodded and swiped a tear from her eye. "It was hauntingly beautiful, and it was meant for you."

I smiled through my tears. "It was, wasn't it?" It wasn't so much that the song was meant for me, but that his words told me that Ryan finally got it. He finally understood my pain. The realization felt even more poignant as the entire restaurant got to its feet and applauded the hometown boys.

"That's gotta be worth at least a conversation," Val joked.

A shadow crossed the table and I knew it was Ryan before I looked up into his hazel eyes. "Hey Pip. Is now a good time to talk?"

I nodded, speechless and accepted Ryan's hand as he led me outside the restaurant and took both of my hands in his. "That song was beautiful, Ryan. But your words? I have none to describe how I feel right now."

His mouth kicked up into a crooked smile. "I'm sorry Pip, that I didn't ask you to come, but you have to know that it wasn't because I didn't love you or didn't want you to come with us, I did. More than anything." He shook his head and let his thumbs glide back and forth over the back of my hand. "I didn't want you to build your life around me. You were always so brilliant at everything you did and I didn't want you putting off your life, your studies and job opportunities for me and the band. I didn't want our life to revolve around my tour schedule, especially if we never made it big."

My heart was so full at his words, so intense and sincere. "I always knew you guys would make it because you worked hard, and most of all, you worked your way up from dive bars and college basement parties."

He blinked. "You knew?"

"You broke my heart, Ryan, but I didn't stop loving you."

He smiled. "What if we hadn't made it big right away Pip? What if we'd spent ten years playing small venues and making no money? You deserved so much more than that."

I nodded at his words that now made so much more sense. "I deserved a chance to decide my own future, Ryan. I deserved the future we dreamed of having. Together."

"I know," he nodded and released my hands to run them through his already disheveled hair. "That's why I'm sorry, but the thought of becoming one of your regrets, I just wasn't strong enough to endure that. In trying to avoid that, I became one anyway."

"Only because I loved you with all of my heart."

"I still love you, Pip. More than I was even capable of loving you back then, because now I know what it's like to live without you and it's hell. I want my days and my nights filled with you. I want you to experience being on tour with us for a few days and I want to learn how to change a diaper."

"You do?" I laughed. "Because that can totally be arranged when you're home."

"Hell yeah. I want the full fatherhood experience from dirty diapers to baby puke and late night feedings. And watching you feed our baby is at the top of that list."

I rolled my eyes. "Still obsessed with my boobs, Ry?"

His grin lit up his whole face. "Still the best boobs around, Pip." He brushed a soft kiss against my lips. "I love you Pip and I mean it, and I'm not letting you go ever again. Not if you love me too. Not if you can forgive me for being a stupid boy in love with a girl still out of his league."

I couldn't help it, I laughed again and it felt real and good. Almost like old times. "I forgive you Ryan. I forgive you because I love you, because my heart has always belonged to you." I aimed a finger at him. "Don't make me regret it."

"Never," he promised with a smile. "I promise that

I will do everything in my power to put a smile on your beautiful face every damn day for the rest of our lives."

"That's a lot of smiling," I said with a laugh.

"Smiles usually come with laughter and there's only one sound in the world I love more than your laughter." He wiggled his eyebrows and just as he planned, I laughed.

"If you're good, maybe you'll get to hear that sound tonight."

He growled and the sound hardened my nipples and dampened my panties. "I look forward to it, but first I want to ask you a question. A very important question." He pulled a single ring from his pocket, except there was nothing simple about it. It was at least two carats, possibly more, emerald cut with a thousand tiny diamonds surrounding it. It was ridiculous and it was stunning. "Pippa Carson, wild girl and incredible woman of my dreams, will you hitch your wagon to mine and enjoy the rest of this journey we call life together?"

It was a perfectly Ryan proposal and I nodded my acceptance before reality set in. "Isn't this too soon?"

"Sweetheart, this is Tennessee and you're carryin' my baby, not mention the small matter of us being madly in love, I'd say is well past time we got married and got on with the rest of our lives. Don't you?"

Did I? I nodded as the answer came swiftly and with

a wide smile. "Hell yes, I do. I can't wait to marry you, Ryan Gregory."

"Why wait?" His lips crashed down on mine before I could answer and I was so giddy, so filled with love that I couldn't help the nervous laughter that bubbled up between us. The kiss was the end of something and the beginning of something even better.

The past was behind us and our future lay in front of us, wide open.

I was a forty year old pregnant bride to be. Anything could happen, and I couldn't wait to see what lay in store next.

The End.

Let me know what you thought of Pippa & Ryan's story

PREVIEW: MIDLIFE FAKE OUT

She was the one with the bottomless brown eyes that always seemed to be on the verge of tears that never fell.

Those eyes had called upon all of my protective instincts.

But that had been too much responsibility for a high school boy.

I hadn't wanted or needed that kind of responsibility.

So I'd rebelled against those instincts, and did the opposite of protecting her.

I bullied her.

PROLOGUE

Derek – *2 Months Ago*

A buzzing sound started to my left, and I flipped over to get the hell away from it. I didn't know what time it was, but the fact that I was still sleeping after the most epic awards show after-party meant it was too damn early for phone calls. But the buzzing didn't stop, and worst of all, there was a cold spot on my bed where a really hot model should have been. My eyes snapped open and I pushed off the bed, scanning the room for any trace of Sasha, or Satya, or something equally as trendy.

"Hello?"

Silence met me as the phone continued to ring. The bedroom floor no longer held a pair of tiny panties. Sheer tiny panties, if I recalled correctly, and I usually did recall, because I wasn't the kind of guy to forget what type of lingerie I tore off with my teeth. Names and jobs? Sure. To call? Almost certainly. But never lingerie. Ever.

I hurried out of the bedroom and down the hall where my black slacks sprawled across the top three steps. I distinctly remembered a long green dress with sparkles on it being somewhere near the bottom of the staircase, but now it was gone too. So were the sky high heels that capped off the longest set of legs I had ever seen. I went left at the bottom of the staircase, and the coffee table still held a half-empty bottle of champagne, two glasses beside it, one stained with a red lipstick imprint. My jacket was on the back of the sofa, along with the bowtie I'd left to hang around my bare chest, because that's what people expected of Derek Gregory, the heartbreaker of The Gregory Brothers trio. Ryan was the moody and sensitive songwriter, and Roman, as the youngest, was the goofball bad boy. We all had our roles, and I'd played mine perfectly for decades now.

I retraced my steps towards the kitchen, which was of course empty, because everyone knew models didn't eat. But there was a note. I smiled and strolled over to the counter.

"Thanks for a good time, Derek. You more than lived up to the hype. *Xoxo – Sascha.*"

I smiled even wider because she was a perfect woman. Looking for a good time with no strings and no expectations, and gone before the awkward morning after, where I would have to explain that I wasn't looking for anything serious, while a woman stared at me with tears swimming in her eyes.

"So did you Sascha, so did you."

In the big empty Nashville mansion, the only sound was my stupid phone still buzzing upstairs on my nightstand.

I took the stairs two at a time, wondering if Ryan or Roman had found themselves in the wrong type of trouble, which rarely happened, but rarely wasn't never. I quickened my steps at the thought that it could be something wrong with our father, GG, or worse, our sister Lacey, who recently decided to become an investigative journalist covering stories in chaotic regions of the world.

"Yeah, what is it?"

A familiar sigh sounded down the line, and I pinched the bridge of my nose a moment before my agent, Brody's angry voice sounded. "So you haven't been abducted by aliens or models, and you're not lying dead on the side of the road," he grumbled. "I guess I should thank the lord for tiny favors. Very tiny."

I rolled my eyes because I knew that tone. "What did I do now?" Usually I managed to balance the line between lovable bad boy and asshole perfectly, but sometimes I stepped over that line. Sometimes I jumped over it by a mile. "Well?"

"You mean other than offending our core audience

with some attempt at comedy that just came off as sexism and misogyny? Is that not enough for you, Derek?"

"You're going to have to give me more details, because all I did last night was accept a few awards, dance all night, and made Sascha moan my name until the wee hours of the morning. So tell me Brody, how have I offended our beloved fans?"

"Stop me when this starts to sound familiar yeah? *She needs to be barefoot and pregnant soon, so you can get her back in the kitchen where she belongs.*"

I froze at those very familiar words. "Yeah they're familiar. I sent that exact text to my new brother-in-law. Yesterday. Was my phone hacked? Don't worry I don't keep nudes on there," I assured him with a laugh.

"Derek," he roared over the phone. "You idiot, you beautiful, talented fucking idiot. You didn't send that to your brother in law, you sent it out to your ten million followers."

"Ten? Try twenty-three million, not that I've been counting." I tried to be active on social media, to keep the fans engaged with photos of me and my brothers, me just living my life.

"Even worse. You did hear the words I just read back do you, didn't you? Barefoot and pregnant? In the kitchen where she belongs? To our mostly female fanbase!"

"Brody it's not that big of a deal. I'll explain that it

was a private message and a joke. I'll even do a video with my sister to show them." This will blow over in a day or two, it always did.

"No you won't. I don't want you to do a goddamn thing Derek, except what I tell you to do. What I need for you to do is go away. Just for a little while. Lay low and go on a social media hiatus until I tell you otherwise."

"What? You've got to be kidding me, Brody. It was just a joke!"

"It was the wrong type of joke at the wrong time, and it offended *everyone*! Go back to that Podunk town you're from and keep a low profile, Derek. Can you do that? For the sake of your career, and if not yours, then your brothers."

"Shit, you're serious."

"Yeah Derek, I'm serious. This whole situation is serious, and I need you to take it seriously."

I worked too hard on my career to lose it now over some silly joke. "I'm listening. Go home and stay away from the spotlight." My shoulders fell in disappointment. "Anything else?"

"No," he sighed in relief. "I need to get with the public relations team and figure out how in the hell to fix this mess. Don't do anything until you hear from me. Got it?"

"Got it."

There must have been something in my tone, because when Brody spoke next, his tone had softened.

"This isn't the end of the world Derek, but it will take some finesse to handle it. Just sit tight, and for once in your life, do as you're told. Tell me you can do that."

"I can do that Brody. My career means everything to me, you know that."

"I do, but I also know you're a stubborn asshole when you want to be."

"I'll close up the house now and head to Carson Creek today," I told him, completely defeated.

"Good. And stay away from all press and social media for the next few days, will you?"

I nodded even though he couldn't see me and dropped down onto my bed. Either that or my legs gave out as the gravity of the situation settled on my shoulders.

"Yeah, okay. Sure." I ended the call and sat on my bed for what felt like forever, contemplating how in the hell I'd ended up here after such a spectacular night.

We'd won three awards last night for our last album, including Song of the Year, and today here I was.

Exiled.

CHAPTER 1
BELLA

Early mornings were my favorite time of day, always had been. The world was quiet and peaceful as the earth tilted to meet the sun's golden rays, and only a few brave souls were awake to see the first beauty of the day. It was, and had always been a private time, a time for me to gather my thoughts and prepare for the day ahead.

Now that I was officially a farmer—again—of my own free will this time, early mornings and to do lists were a necessity. For now I was a one woman operation with the help of a barely teenage boy, who was now, technically, my son.

It hurt to think about Nicola's premature death. She was my best friend, my sister in all but the biological sense, and now she was gone thanks to that unforgiving bitch known as cancer. Her death had left me and her son Everest alone in the world, forced to cope without her sunny disposition and ability to see the positive in any situation. Now it was just us, two cynics who still hadn't found a way to do more than exist without her.

That's what Carson Creek was for. It was meant to be a change, a reset for both of us, but more of a homecoming for me. I grew up here in this town and on this farm. I tilled and watered the land, fed the animals, plucked the crops and sold them all over the state. I loved farm life, it was in my blood, and I'd always dreamed of taking over the place once Ma and Pa retired. Then high school started, and the bullying, the name calling, the stares and the pointing. What fifteen year old girl didn't want to wear makeup and look pretty for hormonal teenage boys, right? Even worse than my distinct lack of desire to impress said boys, my sister would argue that I went out of my way to make sure they weren't interested, but the truth was you could only wash your hands so many times to get the dirt from under your nails. Too many hours in the barn, and not even two showers could completely shake the smell of hay. And what was so wrong with the scent of hay anyway? Without it we wouldn't have food and nourishment, but that only made me more of an outcast.

So instead of sticking around and taking over York Farm, I hightailed it out of this town as fast as I could and claimed the college scholarship that waited for me in Texas, where I'd met my best friend, Nicola.

And now she's gone.

My phone beeped and the screen lit up to remind me that quiet time was over. "Ev, breakfast is ready!" I called upstairs to the sleeping teenager, because I'd learn one month into our first nine months together that yelling was more effective than a gentle shake to wake him from his slumber. The boy slept like the dead, a skill I envied each and every day. I waited and stared at the ceiling until movement stirred above me, before I finished my coffee.

Ten minutes later Everest made his appearance. At just thirteen, he was already the same height as me. But he was at that stage where his limbs were the size of a grown man's, but he was still very much a boy, with long gangly limbs, thick shaggy black hair that looked like it hadn't seen a comb in six months, and skin as smooth and as clear as a baby's. His mother's gray eyes stared back at me, and I couldn't help but smile at the heartbreaker in training.

"You're staring again, Aunt Bella."

"Yeah, I know, and I'm not sorry at all. I was just thinking that one day soon you're going to be such a handsome stinker." He already had the makings of it, and when his growth spurt hit and his baby fat melted away, young adult women of the world would lose their minds.

Everest smirked back at me, a blush stained his cheeks. "Yeah? What am I *now*, chopped liver?"

"Nah, I wouldn't say that. Right now you're a cute stinker, emphasis on stinker. Hungry?"

"Always," he laughed and grabbed the coffee pot.

"Still too young for this," I reminded him.

Everest shrugged and poked his head into the fridge where he emerged with a bottle of orange juice. "Better?"

"Water would be better, but that is acceptable."

"Water isn't going to give me the energy I need for a long day working the fields." It was a good attempt at a guilt trip, but it wasn't good enough.

I laughed and put one hand on my hip. "Working the fields? Hardly, more like feeding some animals and cleaning some stalls, which shouldn't take more than a few hours. When you're done you can go into town and see about making some friends." We'd been in Carson Creek for a few months now, and he'd barely left the farm or made an effort to mingle with the other teens in the area.

His shoulders stiffened at my words. "I don't need to make any friends, Aunt Bella. I'm fine here on the farm. I like it here."

I nodded, because I understood the urge to hide in the face of grief. "This is your home, Ev. You will always belong here, and that won't change if you go out and make a few friends. Have a little fun."

"Not yet, Aunt B. Okay?"

I nodded. "Okay, not yet then. But soon. You don't

want to start school as the new kid."

"Fall is months away. I'll be fine."

"Okay fine. If you'd rather spend time with your super cool aunt, instead of swimming with girls at the lake or sneaking beers at the movie theater, who am I to argue?" I laughed when he rolled his eyes, enjoying this time together, because I knew that one day soon, he would wake up and view me as the enemy.

"You know if this whole farming thing doesn't work out you might have a second career as a standup comic."

"Har-har. Thanks for the vote of confidence, kiddo." I pressed a kiss to his cheek and ruffled his hair before I grabbed my phone and headed towards the back door. "I'll be fixing the fence on the south end for most of the morning, and I have my phone. Take yours with you, just in case." I called instructions over my shoulder for what felt like the hundredth time, and then I was gone, out in the already warm and sunny day.

I smiled as I hopped in my shiny blue pickup truck and headed to the fence that probably hadn't been fixed since the last York left the farm about ten years ago. It was good to be back on the farm, this time around I was older, and supposedly wiser. I didn't need to make friends or connections for my social development, I'd given up on love well before the ink dried on my second divorce, which meant I only had to do two things in this world, raise Everest into a good man, and make this farm a success again.

Both jobs were daunting, and I wasn't even sure I had it in me to do either one of them well, but those were the only things I wanted to do, which meant failure was not an option.

I had a plan. For York Farm and for Everest.

The farm was the easier task to tackle, so I focused on that while I grabbed pliers and twisted the wire around the wood posts, replacing as necessary. The land was big by family farm standards, but there was enough room to grow squash, soybeans and tomatoes on the main plots. Eggs from the chickens would sell well, because they always did, and if the trees on the west end of the property were still good, maybe apples and cider in the fall. The vertical farming buildings were already producing, so the farm could start making a profit sooner rather than later, which would help replenish the money I'd spent to fix this place up and make it livable for me and Everest.

I had a stack of parenting books in my nightstand drawer. Admittedly, that wasn't the most exciting thing to have in that particular drawer, but the books were a greater necessity than battery operated lovers. I now realized that audio books might have been better, since most of my time was spent outdoors, and that way I could multi-task, learn the best ways to parent a child who'd lost his mother, while catching up on my never-ending to-do list.

Mending the farm fence was a hell of a lot easier

than the other fence I would have to mend someday. I wasn't much of a fence-mender in the real world, more of a fence burner. Hell, even that wasn't accurate. The truth was that I was more of a barn burner, I didn't just burn the bridge, I blew up the entire structure. It was my modus operandi because life was easier to deal with that way. Scorched earth meant there was nothing to return to, or attempt to fix later.

"What a joke," I muttered as I examined my handiwork. The fence looked good, but it was the only fence likely to actually get mended. At some point in the future, before I die, I would have to reach out to my four siblings, Abel, Amara, Andora and Alex, and do something or say something. Maybe an apology or something, I didn't have a clue what would do the trick, which meant it wasn't important enough to make it onto my to-do list.

Yet.

Everest likely needed more family than just me, and I had family members in abundance. Maybe the York family could be for him what they had never been for me. Or maybe I just hadn't given them a chance.

I guess my family would go on the list sooner rather than later.

Some days being the adult, the logical and reasonable one, really sucked.

CHAPTER 2
DEREK

It hadn't taken long for boredom to set in once I got back to Carson's Creek. I lasted one week staying with Ryan and Pippa. They were disgustingly in love and I was happy for them, but I didn't need to see my brother and sister-in-law making out while trying to enjoy my morning coffee. And my niece Ryanna was as cute as they came, but she was curious as hell, and when she couldn't explore she proved to have Gregory lungs.

Roman's place was empty, so I stayed there for a few nights since I'd sold my house in Carson Creek last year. That was a good decision at the time, since I didn't spend much time in my hometown, and when I did, I had three siblings and an ornery father to stay with. But my current stay in Carson's Creek wasn't quite working out as I had hoped. After one too many eager groupies showed up at my baby brother's door, I knew my social media restriction wouldn't last long.

So I did what any reasonably wealthy and completely exiled rock star would do.

I bought a farm. Or was it a ranch? It was a giant plot of land with several smaller buildings on it that I hadn't bothered to look into as carefully as my business manager would have liked. It was out on the outskirts of town, which made it perfect in terms of privacy, and there was enough room that I could probably turn one of the buildings into a studio. This exile might be the perfect time to start building my credentials as a producer, at least that's what I told myself, but seven weeks in, and I hadn't even called a contractor. Or hired anyone to tend to the overgrowth which was out of this world.

I thought about asking my neighbors next door, since the rumor in town was that someone had actually purchased or rented the York Farm, but I hadn't seen any evidence of their existence beyond a shiny truck and crops growing day by day. *Great, they were actual farmers,* which probably meant early to bed and early to rise.

The neighborly thing, the southern thing to do, would be to go over there and introduce myself. Maybe offer some muscle once in a while and hope they would do the same for me.

Another time, maybe. I needed, no, I wanted to get the studio built as soon as possible. It would give me something to do, and it would keep me out of trouble until Brody reached out to say I could make trouble again, and do it publicly. I got up and dumped my lukewarm coffee down the sink, I then went about my daily ritual of discreetly checking the internet to see if the women of the world still hated me, and—yep—they did. Instead of stewing over it and cursing the world for my bad luck, I headed outside, determined to scope out the perfect studio space.

The building closest to the main house would be ideal for convenience, but I could put in a small unpaved path if one of the other buildings proved better suited. It was so quiet that I could hear mosquitoes whizzing by my ears, birds chirping in the distance, even the crunch of overgrown foliage under my boots.

It was too quiet.

But I heard a vehicle in the distance, close enough that it was either a visitor for me, or someone at the York Farm was out and about.

My phone beeped with a message from Roman. *"Where the hell are you?"*

"I'm at home. Grounded."

That's exactly what it felt like. I was back to being fourteen and forced to sit in my room and do nothing, not one damn thing, because I'd gotten caught doing something stupid. *Some things don't change*, I thought and smiled to myself.

"We're here," was the next message that came through.

I made my way back to the front of the main house, an act that took even longer than walking the property of my Nashville mansion. Both of my brothers stood on the front porch looking around at the property, probably wondering what in the hell I was thinking.

"Hey, what are you guys doing here?" Not that I wasn't happy to see them, but I hadn't had any visitors in weeks. "Didn't even know you were in town," I told Roman.

Ryan shrugged and ran a hand through his long blond hair with a sheepish smile. "Pippa thought you might be going nuts out here by yourself and made me come."

"Gee, thanks man." I snorted and punched his shoulder.

"I would've come out if you had asked, but you're not exactly the begging type." He wasn't wrong. I didn't need a group to amuse myself, at least that's what I told myself, but I had been going a little stir-crazy out here on my own.

Roman shrugged and clapped me on the back with a playful smile as he gestured to the land before us. "I just wanted to lay eyes on the old hovel, see what kind of dumbass trouble you got yourself into now."

"It's hardly a hovel," I told him and shoved my elbow into his side. "The place just needs some tender loving care, which I plan to give it. With the help of a landscaper and a contractor." Even as I said the words, a vision of what the place would look like came to me.

"A contractor?" Ryan's arched brows nearly disappeared into his hairline. "For what exactly?"

I nodded for them to follow me around to the back of the house. "Afraid I'm going to open up a place to rival Dark Horse?"

"Hell no," he growled. "Nina is happy where she is, so anyone you could get would be a poor imitation."

I rolled my eyes. Nina was a damn fine chef and woman, but I had no desire to run a restaurant. "I'm going to turn one of the buildings into a studio, produce more tracks, maybe some albums for other artists. What do you think?" My brothers and I were close, very close, but we weren't the touchy feely sort to talk about our feelings until our voices went hoarse.

Ryan grinned. "Yeah? That's a good idea. Plus, the main house is big enough if you want to put the artists up yourself."

I hadn't thought about that, but it wasn't a bad idea. "Like those old artist communes back in the day," I mused, suddenly liking the idea more and more.

Roman snorted. "Of course you would decide to do this after my first album is done and on the shelves. But it's a good idea, a good way to keep busy until your current shit storm blows over."

"Don't remind me," I grunted. "One little mistake

and I'm being tarred and feathered." I still couldn't believe it, and I was pissed off. But I promised Brody I would be smart and that I would listen. "Anyway..." I said in search of a change of topic and coming up empty.

"Meet the new neighbors yet?" Ryan asked with a smirk.

"Nope. I guess they're real farmers or something." I did think it was strange that I hadn't even caught a glimpse of them yet. "Or vampires, possibly ghosts."

Ryan rolled his eyes. "Pippa was right, you are going crazy."

"Maybe the ghost farmers are just good at hiding from the misogynistic rock star," Roman mused and pointed to a figure off in the distance.

I followed the direction of his finger and let out a small gasp, because it was an actual person. "Unbelievable." I guess I had started to believe the place might be empty. Carson Creek specialized in gossip, but they didn't always get it right.

"Let's go introduce ourselves," Roman said and started towards the fence before anyone else had agreed. Typical youngest kid, always did whatever the hell he wanted.

"I guess we're going to meet the neighbors," Ryan said with a knowing smile that normally would have set me on edge, but nothing in my life was normal right now and it was all because of social media.

No, it was my fault. Plain and simple.

By the time we got to the fence Roman had already introduced himself, though it probably wasn't necessary because the kid already knew him.

"Oh wow. I love The Gregory Brothers, but your new album is incredible. Been listening to it on a loop since it came out," the teenager with black floppy hair had an awestruck grin.

Roman stood a little taller at the compliment. "I would offer a signed CD, but I wouldn't even know where in the hell, um heck, to get a CD anymore. But I'll definitely get something to you."

The kid laughed and shrugged. "You don't have to do that."

"You kidding? Without fans I wouldn't be shit, I mean hell," he sighed and scrubbed a hand over his face. "You know what I mean right kid?"

"Yeah," he nodded. "I do. The name is Everest, by the way." He finally noticed me and then Ryan with wide gray eyes. "Holy shit, do you guys live next door?"

"I do," I told him and stepped forward with a handshake. "I'm Derek, and I just bought the place. Haven't seen anyone next door at all."

Everest nodded and glanced at the property with a critical eye. "What are you planning to do with the land?"

"My first plan is to get the land cleaned up so I can see what my options are, but I'm going to turn one of the buildings into a recording studio."

"Cool," he nodded and looked around. "I can help clear the land if you want."

"Yeah?" I didn't know, given the current state of things, if that was such a good idea. "Why?"

He shrugged. "My aunt keeps talking about going into town and making friends. If I have something else to do, especially a job, she might lay off awhile longer."

I frowned. "You don't want to make friends?" What kind of teenager didn't want friends, especially a good looking kid like him that could easily be very popular?

"I just got here, and things have been rough. My mom passed away, and I'm just taking it easy for a while." He scanned the grounds once again and turned to me with those gray eyes that looked as if they'd seen too much. "I spotted some peach trees on the south end of your property, if you're interested in tending them, they look to be bearing fruit." The way the kid breezed over the dead mom information called to me, I'd done the same when we lost our mother.

I smiled at his mature way of speaking. "You grew up on a farm?"

"Nah, but my aunt did, and she knows all kinds of stuff."

"So why aren't you helping her?" Roman shoved his hands in his pockets and leveled Everest with a look.

"She only lets me feed the animals and clean their living areas because she wants to make sure she can handle the workload when I become the most popular kid in town." He snorted his opinion at that aspiration. "Anyway, you know where I'll be if you decide you want some help. It's a big job."

We all smirked at how easy the kid was with us. "Everest, why did you guys choose Carson Creek?" There were bigger towns and bigger farms throughout the state.

He shrugged at first, and then lifted his eyes to the blue sky and blinding sun. "She grew up here. Said she didn't much like it here back then, but that it was a great place for us both to start over, so here we are. Oh and this is her family's farm."

No. it couldn't be. The universe couldn't be so cruel to me, not now when I was exiled to my hometown. The universe would not trap me beside my biggest regret, would it?

There were five York kids, and three of them were girls. It could just as easily be Andora or Amara, but my gut knew that it wasn't. It was the svelte York sister, the one with the bottomless brown eyes that always seemed to be on the verge of tears that never fell. Those eyes had called upon all of my protective instincts. But that had been too much responsibility for a high school boy. I hadn't wanted or needed that kind of responsibility. So I'd rebelled against those instincts, and did the opposite of protecting her.

I had bullied her. Badly.

"One of the York girls," Ryan mused. "Which one?"

"Bella York," a rich feminine voice answered as she

came to a stop beside Everest. She was as beautiful as ever. Gorgeous with her long limbs, strong and lean. Her white tank top showed off her shoulders and toned arms, a pink bra peeked from behind one of the straps. But her legs were the real superstars, encased in denim that looked damn near painted on. A floppy hat sat on top of her thick brown hair that hung halfway down her back, or would have if the wind hadn't picked it up and swirled it around her body. She put a hand on Everest's shoulder and smiled. "The Gregory Brothers. Hey Ryan. Roman." She didn't say my name or even look in my direction, and I wasn't at all surprised.

"Bella York," Roman purred and leaned in with an appreciative smile. "You always were a pretty thing, but holy hell woman. I'm of legal age now," he reminded her and wiggled his eyebrows.

Bella laughed, and the sound was thick and rich. "Thanks Roman. And congratulations on your solo and group success. You guys are all over the place."

"We took a risk, and it paid off." Ryan shrugged like it was no big deal. "What are you planning to grow?"

"Quite a bit actually. Soybeans will be our biggest crop, there will also be squash and tomatoes, and hopefully some apples from the orchard. I also have a vertical farm with plenty of herbs and leafy greens. A lot of stuff," she said with an embarrassed laugh. "Sorry."

"Don't be," Ryan assured her. "I own Dark Horse, it's

a high end restaurant in town, and my chef Nina loves to come out and pick fresh food. She would love this."

I watched as she chatted easily with my brothers, and wondered to myself how it was possible that she had gotten even prettier over the years. She was still willowy with this innately delicate look about her, but now there was also a strength about her, inside and out. "It was great to see you guys, a real blast from the past. But I need to get back to it," she said and thumbed in the direction over her shoulder. "Tell your chef to come by anytime to check the place out. I'm happy to show her around." She took a few steps back, brown eyes smiling wide at my brothers before she turned to Everest with an affectionate smile.

"What about me?" I shouldn't have said anything. I should have just left it well enough alone. She didn't like me, probably hated me, and she had good reason to ignore me completely. But that just wasn't my style.

Annabella York froze and turned slowly to level me with an icy glare. "What about you?"

I took a step forward and licked my lips. "Am I welcome anytime?"

She flashed a sexy smile, and I swore my knees gave out a little. She was hot as hell fully clothed, and I couldn't help but imagine what she would look like in nothing at all.

"You, Derek Gregory are welcome, never. Not ever, even if there's an end of the world disaster. Unless of course you have a fondness for the taste and feel of shotgun slugs."

"Ouch," Roman groaned and then laughed.

With a pointed look at me to make sure I got the hint, she turned and walked away, long legs eating up the space quickly.

My brothers roared with laughter at her insult, looking at me with questions in their eyes that I refused to answer. "I can't wait to hear that story," Ryan said around a loud guffaw.

Even Everest laughed. "Wow. I'm pretty sure Aunt Bella hates you, and she likes everyone. *Everyone*," he emphasized. "Sorry," he added with a shrug. "It was nice to meet you guys. All of you." He waved and walked off, shaking his head with an amused smile.

As soon as Everest was out of earshot, Roman laughed even more loudly. "What the hell was that about man?"

"Ancient history," I growled and walked away from the fence, putting as much distance between me and Bella York as possible. With her so close, her hatred so palpable, it didn't feel all that ancient. It just felt like another thing that I would have to apologize for.

Eventually.

Some day.

Later.

Bella & Derek's story continues in Midlife Fake Out.

Also by Piper Sullivan

Midlife Fake Out: Bella & Derek

Midlife Love Story: Carlotta & Chase

Midlife Love Affair: Lacy & Levi

Midlife Valentine: Valona & Trey

Midlife Do Over: Pippa & Ryan

Healing Love

Dueling Drs, Book 6: Zola & Drew

Rockstar Baby Daddy, Book 5: Susie & Gavin

Unfriending the Dr, Book 4: Persy & Ryan

Kissing the Dr, Book 3: Megan & Casey

Loving the Nurse, Book 2: Gus & Antonio

Falling for the Dr, Book 1: Teddy & Cal

Curvy Girl Dating Agency

Forever Curves, Book 8: Brenna & Grant

Small Town Curves, Book 7: Shannon & Miles

Curvy Valentine Match, Book 6: Mara & Xander

Misbehaving Curves, Book 5: Joss & Ben

Curves for the Single Dad, Book 4: Tara & Chris

His Curvy Best Friend, Book 3: Sophie & Stone

Curvy Girl's Secret, Book 2: Olive & Liam

His Curvy Enemy, Book 1: Eva & Oliver

Small Town Protectors (Tulip Series)

That Hot Night, Book 12: Janey & Rafe

To Catch A Player, Book 11: Reece & Jackson

Cold Hearted Love, Book 10: Ginger & Tyson

Hero Boss, Book 9: Stevie & Scott

Dr's Orders, Book 8: Maxine & Derek

Mastering Her Curves, Book 7: Mikki & Nate

Kissing My Best Friend, Book 6: Bo & Jase

Undesired, Book 5: Hope & Will

Wanting Ms Wrong, Book 4: Audrey & Walker

Loving My Enemy, Book 3: Elka & Antonio

Bad Boy Benefits, Book 2: Penny & Ry

Hero In My Bed, Book 1: Nina & Preston

Accidental Hookups

Accidentally Hitched, Book 1: Viviana & Nash

Accidentally Wed, Book 2: Maddie & Zeke

Accidentally Bound, Book 3: Trish & Mason

Accidentally Wifed, Book 4: Magenta & Davis

Boardroom Games

His Takeover: An Enemies to Lovers Romance (Boardroom Games Book 1)

Sinful Takeover: An Enemies to Lovers Romance (Boardroom Games Book 2)

Naughty Takeover: An Enemies to Lovers Romance (Boardroom Games 3)

Boxsets & Collections

Small Town Misters: A Small Town Protectors Boxset

Misters of Pleasure: A Small Town Protectors Boxset

Misters of Love: A Small Town Romance Boxset

Misters of Passion: A Small Town Romance Boxset

Kiss Me, Love Me: An Alpha Male Romance Boxset

Accidentally On Purpose: A Marriage Mistake Boxset

Daddies & Nannies: A Contemporary Romance Boxset

Cowboys & Bosses: A Contemporary Romance Boxset

About the Author

Piper Sullivan is an old school romantic who enjoys reading romantic stories as much as she enjoys writing them.

She spends her time day-dreaming of dashing heroes and the feisty women they love.

Visit Piper's website www.pipersullivan.com

Join Piper's Newsletter for quirky commentary, new romance releases, freebies and contests.

Check her out on BookBub

Stalk her on Facebook

Printed in Dunstable, United Kingdom